Silent Heart

Claire McNab

Bella
BOOKS

2005

Bella Books, Inc.
P.O. Box 10543
Tallahassee, FL 32302

First published 1993 by Naiad Press

Printed in the United States of America on acid-free paper
First Edition

Editor: Katherine V. Forrest
Cover designer: Sandy Knowles

ISBN 1-59493-044-9

For Sheila

About the Author

CLAIRE MCNAB is the author of fifteen Detective Inspector Carol Ashton mysteries: *Lessons in Murder, Fatal Reunion, Death Down Under, Cop Out, Dead Certain, Body Guard, Double Bluff, Inner Circle, Chain Letter, Past Due, Set Up, Under Suspicion, Death Club, Accidental Murder* and *Blood Link*. She has written two romances, *Under the Southern Cross* and *Silent Heart*, and has co-authored a self-help book, *The Loving Lesbian*, with Sharon Gedan. She is the author of four Denise Cleever thrillers, *Murder Undercover, Death Understood, Out of Sight,* and *Recognition Factor*.

An Australian now living permanently in Los Angeles, she teaches fiction writing in the UCLA Extension Writers' Program. She makes it a point to return once a year to Australia to refresh her Aussie accent.

CHAPTER ONE

The water at Circular Quay sparkled in Sydney's relentless summer light. The Opera House's huge curved shells looked suitably impressive for any tourist. The waiter slid a plate in front of me with reverent precision. Hugh Oliver of Rampion Press beamed at me across the table, his high color and short sandy hair giving the impression of a mischievous and somewhat overweight schoolboy.

I feigned enthusiasm. "I'm very much looking forward to the States . . ."

This is what two-thirds of my lunch-time

audience wanted to hear. "It'll be a humdinger of an author tour!" said Hugh with all the enthusiasm appropriate for the head of Rampion's publicity department. Christie O'Keefe, photographer, nodded affirmation. The third person at the table just looked at me.

I stared back, masking the hostility I felt. Reyne Kendall was a journalist published internationally by *Millennium* magazine. Hugh Oliver had taken all the credit for organizing the article that was to feature me and, more importantly, my book, *The Erotic Muse*. He had called me two days ago, his self-satisfied voice booming over the line. "I'm so pleased, Victoria, that the editor has run with my idea . . . and that he's going the whole hog. The *Millennium* article won't just be a page or two, but an in-depth piece with color photographs in all editions, American and international." He had then cajoled me into lunch with the photographer and journalist assigned to the story.

So here I was, sitting in a charming restaurant with a stunning view of city and harbor, looking at a woman who, in my normal life, I would never even consider meeting. Reyne Kendall was of average height, strongly built, and even when motionless, had an aura of energy. Her gestures were sudden, definite, her manner disdainful. Her brown hair was enlivened with a hint of red, her eyebrows emphatic, her eyes dark, she had an unexpected dimple when she smiled. When still, her face was solemn, unremarkable, but animation gave her an attractiveness that flared beneath her fair skin.

From our first meeting an hour or so before, she'd been the brash, aggressive journalist I'd expected. Full of opinions, questions, cynical observations, all delivered in a voice that was too loud, too confident. When Hugh had first suggested the luncheon, I'd reviewed the little I knew about the woman and then consigned her to a mental box labeled "journalist-reporter, blunt, ambitious, exploitative." Up to this point she'd fitted the stereotype, and my initial wariness had ripened into active dislike. I felt justified in my evaluation of her. Now she was unsettling me with her silence, her level stare measuring me dispassionately.

My expression must have shown something, because she said abruptly, "You've absolutely no idea what you're letting yourself in for, Professor."

I was sure she used my title with irony, as I'd been introduced as Victoria Woodson. Before I could respond, Hugh, predictably, rushed in. "Reyne, I'm sure Victoria has a very clear idea what's involved — the promotion of a world-wide bestseller!"

"You've got a vested interest in making her think it's a piece of cake." She turned to me with a sardonic smile. "The first thing you learn is never take anyone in publicity seriously."

I said lightly, "I try not to take anything too seriously, and that naturally includes Hugh."

"You surprise me," said Reyne. "I'd have thought you might tend to take *everything* rather too seriously."

My aversion to this woman was healthy — and growing. I turned away from her to say to Christie O'Keefe, "You said you wanted to take a few quick photographs with the Opera House in the background. How about now, while we're waiting for coffee?"

I was warming to Christie. We had chatted effortlessly through lunch and I appreciated her self-deprecating humor. I also found her air of unfussy competence much more acceptable than Reyne Kendall's tough reporter persona. Physically, even, Christie was more comfortable. Much shorter than I, she had a pleasant face, pale blonde hair and a slight build. Her taste in clothes tended towards somewhat gaudy primary colors, but she moved with capable economy and impressed me as someone who would always be on time and fulfill her professional duties well.

Leaving Hugh and Reyne debating some trivial matter, Christie and I left the discreet coolness of the restaurant for the strident heat of a summer day. A broad balcony overlooked the busy cove, and while Christie unpacked her well-worn black leather equipment case, I leaned against the railing and contemplated the city. The towers rose, washed by sunlight. A sleek white luxury liner was moored at the International Terminal, ferries hurried to wharfs, the Opera House sat complacent in its bizarre beauty.

"Do you ever wear bright colors?" Christie said as she tried different camera angles.

"Not as a rule. I prefer white, black, navy blue . . ."

Christie grinned at me. "Hey, that's great, but as *Millennium* prints in color, maybe you should consider something that's —"

"Less plain?" I said, eyeing her brilliant red and yellow overalls.

"Uh huh." She laughed as she peered from

4

behind the camera. "I wasn't suggesting the sort of thing I've got on — just something in a warm rose, or maybe a lime green."

I looked down at my white linen skirt and tailored dark blue blouse. Perhaps my taste in clothes was too conservative for someone like Christie, but I felt at ease with my classic style. Wanting to change the subject, I said, "You've worked with Reyne Kendall before?"

"Sure have." Her face alive with amusement, Christie added, "I suspect you two may be evenly matched."

"Oh, yes?"

"Reyne can be intimidating. I don't think she realizes the impression she makes."

I was sure she did, but I nodded affirmatively.

Christie squeezed off several quick shots. "And the fact you're a professor throws her a bit, I think."

"Why?" I was genuinely puzzled.

"She's the classic self-made woman — started at the bottom and did it the hard way. Reyne's got a great track record, learned it all on the job, is suspicious of paper qualifications ..."

"Suspicious? She sounds positively paranoid."

Christie's smile was indulgent. "I'm sure Reyne admires what you've achieved. There's just no way she'll ever admit it — to herself or to you."

"So Ms Kendall doesn't mellow with longer acquaintance?"

"Mellow? Not a word I'd ever associate with Reyne." She moved me along the railing, squinted into the viewfinder. "That's what makes her so good — she's uncompromising, unsentimental, and almost impossible to fool. She's done some great investigative journalism. Did you see her series exposing the scandal of international tax shelters?"

"Don't think I did."

Christie grinned. "The way *The Erotic Muse* is selling, maybe you'll need to study it."

After lunch, as I drove back to the university, I considered with apprehension the disturbance to my ordered life that *The Erotic Muse* had caused. Surely I'd never have agreed to rewriting my academic study if I'd realized what an upheaval it would create . . . But, then again, there was now a tinge of excitement to each day, and I was vain enough to feel pleasure at the public recognition of my name and the fuss that Rampion Press was making over me.

The reaction of my university colleagues to my sudden notoriety had varied. The Vice Chancellor had tut-tutted, but avoided outright condemnation — what he'd actually said was, "Pity there's so much actual *sex* in it, Victoria. Otherwise it's an admirable study, particularly on the hypocrisy in the establishment." Those in my own department had run the gamut in their responses — envy, outrage, amusement, approval. No one was indifferent, including my students, whose contributions to tutorials now included considerably more comments about sex and love. With amusement I'd realized that their former perception of me as a dry, remote professor had been replaced by a somewhat spicier academic model. As I waited for a traffic light to change, my gaze idly fell on a newsstand and the latest *Millennium* magazine. I felt a sudden guilty pride that such an up-market publication would be featuring me. Of course I didn't really deserve it — all I'd done was take the great themes of love and desire in literature and make them accessible to a wider public. I was quite prepared for it all to be an exciting few months of notoriety, then I would sink back into anonymity again.

As vividly as a photograph, Reyne Kendall jumped into my mind, staring at me with insolent, dark eyes. What did she think of me? Had she read my book and sneered at the thought of an associate professor of English cashing in on the constant human interest in sex?

As I considered my almost immediate dislike for her, I vaguely recalled a psychological explanation for the antipathy I felt — something to do with the idea that you recognize in the other person a characteristic that you yourself have, but don't accept. That didn't seem a likely explanation here. Apart from the fact that we were both female, we had nothing else in common. Reyne Kendall was brusque, inquisitive, pushy, whereas I was ...

I smiled to myself. The words I would use included logical, reasonable, controlled — yet here I was on a dizzying merry-go-round of appearances and interviews because I had allowed my academic literary treatise to be transformed into a popular success.

My office at the university wasn't large, but it was neat and well-organized, dominated by an antique desk I'd restored myself, and decorated with a few favorite pictures, mostly etchings of native

7

birds. I opened the door with pleasure, expecting to enjoy the solitude of a few hours of work.

"You're here at last," said Zoe from where she stood at the window.

As usual, my cousin started our conversation by pacing impatiently with small, emphatic steps, her high heels digging viciously into the gray-blue carpet. I'd seen her only a few weeks ago, but she'd noticeably put on weight. Zoe was perpetually on some new diet, each embarked upon with religious fervor, then criticized with bitter disappointment when the loss turned out to be temporary.

Ever since I could remember, Zoe had been able to aggravate me by her refusal to sit still, to listen, to be logical. Always an emotional incendiary device, today she was spitting the words out with righteous outrage. ". . . never considered the family, when you wrote it, did you? *Typical* of you, Victoria. It's a good thing Mum's gone — she'd be *sickened* to see what you've done. And Dad's past it, thank God."

"I haven't *done* anything. It's an academic study."

"Academic?" Zoe always sneered effectively. "It's called *The Erotic Muse,* isn't it? You really think that's an academic title?"

"My publishers —"

"Your *publishers.* How can you look anyone here at the university in the eye after the Rampion Press advertising campaign? You *can't* approve of the ads! They're selling sex, it's simple as that. I don't know what John thinks, but *I* . . ." Her shrug was the distillation of years of displeasure with me, the intruder into her family.

Somehow her antagonism was comfortable. I

8

always knew where I stood with Zoe, having spent my life from age seven learning the rules of the games she played. "I'm sorry if you're upset, Zoe, but I'm not going to apologize for my book or anything to do with it."

"You make me ashamed of the Woodson name."

I was tired of Zoe's extravagances. "You don't even have the Woodson name. You changed it when you married Arthur." I didn't add a comment on the backflip she'd accomplished to do this — from ardent feminist resisting patriarchal social mores to enthusiastic endorser of the status quo.

Mention of her marriage always soothed Zoe. Her tone was more conciliatory as she said, "Don't suppose you chose the title, anyway."

Her comment amused me. I remembered the publishing executive's horror as he exclaimed, "You can't call it *that!*" when I made what I thought was a clear concession by condensing the original title, *A Study in Carnal Affection in Literature from the Victorian to Modern Times* to the snappier *Carnal Affection in Literature.*

"I didn't chose the title," I conceded.

"Suppose it's already made quite a lot of money?"

"I think it might, eventually."

She finally sat down, a move I recognized as a bargaining stance. Zoe was nothing if not predictable. Her first move in this phase was always to show a desultory interest in my personal life. "How's Gerald? You haven't mentioned him lately."

"Gerald's fine."

"Perhaps you two could come round for dinner one night?"

9

"Zoe, I don't think —"

"Don't tell me you've broken up with Gerald! Honestly, Victoria, he's just *perfect* for you."

It was easier to take the path of least resistance. "I'll see when Gerald's free and call you, but it won't be right away. I've got this author tour coming up."

Zoe nodded, satisfied. The preliminaries over, she leaned forward to say earnestly, "You know, Victoria, I must remind you that we are expecting you to invest a little in the family." When I didn't respond, Zoe's lips curled in the charming smile she'd used as a weapon all her life. "Arthur's business has excellent prospects . . ."

Arthur St. James was a thoroughly presentable husband for Zoe, but the very thing that attracted her — his malleability — made him a very inefficient businessman. He was talented in computer software development, but lacked the skills to capitalize on his abilities; his little software company constantly trembled on the brink of disaster, saved only by the genuinely innovative product that he had created, however badly he marketed it.

"Zoe, you should understand that there's a considerable delay before I receive royalties, no matter how well the book is selling."

"Okay, but when you do get paid, I'd like to think you'll put money into Arthur's company."

"I'll consider it."

It used to disconcert me, the way Zoe could change from emotion to emotion, as though a switch had been thrown. Now, I mentally shrugged as she abruptly stood up, her face flooded with instant anger. "We're *family*, Victoria. You owe it to me."

I didn't ask, "Why you, in particular?" I already

knew the answer. Zoe felt she was entitled to reparations. She had been a precocious eight-year-old when I had been thrust into her comfortable world by the death of my parents. To me personally, Zoe had never bothered to hide the bitter resentment she felt towards an orphaned child who had usurped her position as baby of the family. She was more circumspect with others, earning admiration for the loving way she had tried to make her cousin welcome.

I wondered, as I often did, how anyone could choose to live with Zoe, although Arthur seemed content, even happy. Perhaps it was *my* perception that was at fault — I didn't see things the way others did. For example, looking back at my childhood with Zoe, John, and my aunt and uncle, I perceived myself as quiet and cooperative, but I could still hear my Aunt Felice, Zoe's mother, as she repeated her constant observation, "You're a difficult child, Victoria. Very difficult." She had never explained what "difficult" might mean, and her tight-lipped austere face ensured that I never asked her.

Strange how someone with such a soft name — Felice — could be so forbidding, so strict. My aunt was well-matched with her husband, an Anglican minister whose God was definitely Old Testament. My memories of him always included his harsh, metallic voice vibrating with righteous anger. Aunt Felice was a much quieter, but even more formidable person, and though she had died some months ago after her second heart attack, to me her presence was still palpable.

11

I came back to the present with Zoe's impatient, "Well?"

"I'll consider it, that's all I'll say. And don't try to make me feel guilty, Zoe, please."

Zoe had early mastered the ironic impact of one raised eyebrow. "Guilty?" she said, her emphasis making it clear that this would be an appropriate response from me.

Then, abruptly, she was moving towards the door. Zoe always liked to terminate conversations first, whether on the telephone or in person. It used to challenge me to beat her to it, but now it just wasn't important enough to try. She paused. "I almost forgot. I've finally got around to going through some of Mum's things, and I found some photos you might like to have."

When she had closed the door behind her, I sat looking at the brown envelope on my desk. I'd never been sentimental, never kept photographs or keepsakes to remember the past. I didn't believe in looking back.

Reluctantly, I slid out the contents of the envelope. Photographs of me, unsmiling, squinting at the camera. Not one of them taken before I came to my aunt and uncle's cold home. None of my real mother and father. None of the house near the beach that I'd gone back to as an adult and tried, in vain, to remember as part of my early childhood.

I flicked through the family photographs — Zoe smiling vivaciously at the camera, John taking his status as eldest very seriously, Uncle David stern, his white clerical collar as tight as his mouth, Aunt Felice with her careful smile that never showed her teeth. And me — I felt a pulse of anguish at the face of that little girl, hollow-cheeked, grave, staring stoically out at me.

"You're so dramatic," I said to myself as I shuffled the photos together and shoved them back into the envelope, upon which Zoe had written with her impatient scrawl, *For Victoria*. There was no reason for me to feel any particular sorrow for the little girl who had been me. I could remember only snatches of my life before my aunt and uncle took me in, and from then on it wasn't unbearable. I wasn't an emotional child — I didn't wail and complain, and I was looked after well and given educational opportunities that had eventually led to my present position as Associate Professor of English. Really, I had no grounds for reproach.

But still, that thin face that had been me stayed in my mind.

I'd asked Gerald for dinner that evening — or rather, he'd maneuvered me until I gave him the invitation. I watched him warily as he opened the wine for dinner, his long thin fingers skillfully manipulating my skittish corkscrew. He looked serious, preoccupied, and I felt a brush of apprehension about what he might want to discuss.

Tao, my sleek Burmese cat, was contemplating us both, his body tucked into a neat parcel with his paws folded under his chest. I stroked delicately between his ears and was rewarded by the sigh of a purr. "Have a good day?" I said to Gerald, introducing a safely neutral topic. If that subject failed, I could always fall back on the weather.

"The usual. Creative excuses why assorted theses are running late, tutorials where the only students who contribute are the ones who've done no preparation whatsoever, the customary skirmishes with Admin ..." He grinned as the cork came out smoothly. "Pretty much an ordinary day. How about you?"

"Lunch in the City with publisher, photographer and rabid journalist."

Gerald possessed a deceptively mild appearance. I was accustomed to hearing what a nice man he was, expressed in tones of surprise that implied a professor of history could not normally be expected to have this quality. *Nice* was too weak a word to describe him — *civilized* suited him better.

As he poured the wine, he said, "No doubt your publisher was represented by the attentive Hugh Oliver, but who were the others?"

I hadn't enjoyed lunch, and wanted to forget about it. Equally strongly, I didn't want Gerald bringing up anything about our relationship. Deciding to skate over the information and then firmly lead us back to a reliable topic, such as university politics, I said, "Both from *Millennium* magazine. The photographer's an American woman, Christie O'Keefe. The journo's Reyne Kendall."

He surprised me when he said, "Know them both."

"Indeed? Is *Millennium* doing a cover story on Gerald Humphries?"

He grinned at my tone. "No, darling, *you're* the one the magazine's profiling, because you're the one with the sexy bestseller."

The word "darling" reverberated in the room. I

was scrupulous never to use endearments, and his casual use of the term seemed almost to imply ownership.

With his usual care, he settled the wine bottle into its bed of ice in the silver bucket he'd given me for my birthday. "The reason I know Christie O'Keefe is that she collaborated on Penter's book — she did all those moody photographs to match the moody poems." Dr. Penter, from the School of Computing Studies, was an officious, bustling man with an astonishing streak of literary ability in him. "And Reyne Kendall's done some sound work on street kids. Had a lead article a couple of issues ago that I thought was pretty good stuff."

"I didn't see it." I *had* seen it, but couldn't bear to read about the misery of abandoned children's lives.

Gerald was looking at me with a faint smile. "I get the feeling you didn't warm to Reyne Kendall."

"She was confronting, pushy. I'm not looking forward to having her tag along to Brisbane and Melbourne."

"It's the price of fame, Victoria. You better get used to it, especially when you tour the States."

"*If* I tour the States."

My prevarication didn't convince him. "You know the university will give you the time off, and you'll be surprised how quickly you become accustomed to limousines and luxury hotels."

I sipped my wine. It disturbed my ordered world, but it was exciting — to be caught up in a round of interviews, of people wanting to meet me, speak with me, just because I had written a surprise bestseller. I heard Zoe's sharp words: ". . . selling sex, it's as simple as that." She had a way of cheapening things I'd achieved, but I refused to feel ashamed of what I'd written.

"Gerald, I know it's got a catchy title, and I've rewritten some of it for the general public, but..."

He touched my hand reassuringly. "Yes, your book's good, don't ever have any doubts. Good scholarship and good writing, and we both know those two don't necessarily go together." His expression changed. "Talking about going together..."

"I'll check the oven."

He followed me into the kitchen. "We need to talk about us."

I tried to speak lightly. "No we don't. Everything's fine."

"It isn't fine for me."

I felt trapped, smothered by his demanding affection. Allowing anger to defend me, I said sharply, "What more do you want? You've got a companion, a colleague, a bedmate. You're not going to ask me to wash your socks, are you?"

He put his hands on my shoulders. "I want a commitment."

"Oh, come on!"

"Don't dismiss what I'm saying without thinking about it, Victoria. It's what we both need — a permanent relationship."

I had thought about it, long and hard. Keeping my voice level, I said, "I don't need it, Gerald. And if it's a condition of us staying together..."

His short laugh was bitter. "Staying together? We're not together in any way I accept. So, we spend time with each other, we go to bed fairly regularly . . . in your terms that's a relationship, is it?"

"I've got to serve dinner."

Taking the chicken out of the oven gave me an excuse to avoid his accusing gaze, but his tone slapped me. "Jesus, Victoria! How do I get through to you? I care for you — but I don't think you love anyone, not even yourself."

Fury made my voice thick. "Remember history's your forte, Gerald, not psychoanalysis."

He leaned back against the kitchen bench and folded his arms. "Since you've brought it up, why not consider therapy?"

I stared at him. "Therapy? Me? You've got to be joking!"

His face was flushed with anger, but he kept his voice level. "Don't just refuse to consider the idea. It could give you some insight —"

"Into what? Your delicate male ego?"

"How many relationships have you had, Victoria, before me? I'm the last of a long line of men, and you've dropped every one of us the moment things got too intense. I think you've got a problem."

"I have. It's *you*." I wasn't afraid of other people's anger, but my own rage terrified me. I took a deep breath. "I don't want to talk about this."

"We have to."

I wanted to smash something — a plate, a glass, his concerned face. "Gerald, please go."

He was astonished. "Go? But we . . ."

"Take the chicken with you, if you're hungry," I said with bitter humor. "But leave, right now."

He closed the door behind him very gently, as I knew he would. I looked around the room, relief spiraling through me. Relief that I didn't have to go through the motions of a relationship. And, though I shied away from the thought, relief that I didn't have to share my bed tonight.

CHAPTER TWO

Chantrey's Bookshop was awash with people and the hum of conversation. Traffic noise filtered in from the busy city street outside. A long, fairly narrow store, it was organized with shelving that broke the flow, encouraging customers to eddy around strategically placed stacks. The book signing — my first major one — was to be at the end furthest from George Street, where an area had been cleared for a lectern and a microphone and a gaggle of chairs.

As Hugh Oliver, flushed with self-importance, led

the way, I glanced sideways at the large stacks of my book at the entrance. I couldn't get used to seeing my own face staring out from the back cover. Resisting Rampion's blandishments to wear academic dress — "Sex and a mortarboard! The contrast, don't you see?" — I'd finally agreed to what the photographer cheerfully called "a dramatic three-quarter face," the effect achieved by the interplay of light and shadow. I usually wore my long dark hair in a disciplined chignon, but for the photograph it was loose on my shoulders. Light ran along my cheekbones and hollowed my cheeks. To myself, I looked severe, controlled. My mouth was resolute, my hands were folded neatly in my lap. Yet there was a disturbing echo of my former self as I'd been captured in the photograph Zoe had given me the day before.

"Victoria! In here." Hugh shepherded me into a small room used by the staff. "This will be a major appearance. A good dress rehearsal for the States. Do you have your notes ready? Is there anything you want?"

"A gin and tonic."

Hugh looked taken aback, then laughed. "We'll have a celebratory drink afterwards." He swelled a little. "This is going to be a great success — we should get coverage in the press. Did you see the size of the crowd?"

Part of Hugh's enthusiasm had been generated by free publicity. My scheduled appearance had caused a small group of outraged citizens, complete with inflammatory placards, to picket the bookstore early that morning. They had thoughtfully contacted the media to make sure their protests that I was undermining the religious foundations of society would feature in the early news bulletins. The leader had denounced both me and *The Erotic Muse.* "When the seats of higher learning in this country are corrupted . . . when the professors whose duty it is to teach our young are peddling filth . . . when base pornography is viewed as literature . . ." It was the type of publicity that couldn't be bought.

"You didn't set that protest up yourself?" I asked Hugh as he checked the growth of the crowd outside for what seemed the fifteenth time.

Hugh smoothed his sandy hair, as though soothing himself with the motion. "Of course not. Mind you, I suppose it's the success of the pre-publicity for this appearance that encouraged them, so maybe I did have something to do with it — but only indirectly." He caught my dubious expression, and added quickly, "I'd do a lot for publicity, but setting up a fake demonstration would be a bit much."

I wasn't so sure. Early in my association with Rampion Press the company's highly regarded publicity manager had been headhunted by a rival company, and Hugh, as second in command, had leaped into her seat. It was clear that he felt he had to consolidate his position by proving himself equal, if not better, than his predecessor, and the success of the publicity campaign and the sales of my book were a means to that end.

Hugh was beginning to sweat. He wiped his face surreptitiously, straightened his tie and frowned at me. "Victoria, you know Paul Chantrey will be introducing you himself . . . that is, the *younger* Paul Chantrey." Hugh was always delighted to have some tidbit of gossip, so he added, "There's some talk his second marriage to the ballerina's in trouble . . ."

The Chantrey family was an institution in Sydney, having run family-owned bookshops for several generations. Having met Paul Chantrey on several occasions when he'd hosted popular literature seminars at the university, I was impressed by his utter superficiality. I seriously doubted if he'd ever read any of the books he sold — in my opinion, comic books would be a challenge to him.

This was not to say that Chantrey wasn't presentable. Watching him as swept through the door of the staff office, Italian suit immaculate, face lightly tanned, I wondered why he'd never considered politics — he had that telling combination of height, regular features and a semblance of sincerity. Ignoring Hugh's attempts to introduce us, Chantrey said, "Professor! How wonderful to see you again! And what a privilege to have you here at Chantrey's major store . . ." He belonged to that group of people who love to repeat their own names, so he added, "I'd like to think that Chantrey's will always be your first choice when launching your books, Professor Woodson."

And in his introductory speech to the not inconsiderable crowd that had collected at the back of the store, he managed to mention Chantrey at least ten times. ". . . and now, I'm sure you're as delighted as I am to welcome Professor Victoria Woodson to Chantrey's Bookshop . . ."

Some people clapped. Some stared at me with bovine expressions. Alarmingly, a few faces held expressions of fervent, zealous interest. My career had made me relaxed about speaking to groups, large or small, but suddenly a thread of anxiety brushed me. I'd selected a short passage to read, and had my notes, prompts for a graceful little speech about the gratifying interest that publication of the book had generated in the Victorian literary period. Now, looking at my audience, I realized that what I intended to say was inappropriate.

Somebody coughed. Paul Chantrey smiled in anticipation, no doubt, that I would use his name when thanking him. "Good morning," I said, opting for a non-controversial beginning. Over the heads of the people standing at the back I caught sight of Reyne Kendall. She was watching me with clinical detachment, waiting, perhaps, for me to make a fool of myself.

Early that morning, over my usual breakfast of toast and tea, I'd read Reyne's *Millennium* article on street children, rescuing the copy of the magazine from the neat pile I had ready for paper recycling. I was right to have avoided the article before — it made me wince and, finally, moved me to tears. In her writing I saw a Reyne Kendall that surprised me. Probing, unsentimental, unbiased — yet keenly feeling the human cost of children our society had failed. And she used words well, writing supple, strong prose that caught and held attention.

Thinking this, I smiled at her, and was rather unkindly amused when she was clearly disconcerted.

Abandoning my notes, I gave a series of brief readings from my book on the subject of "the first kiss."

Aware that some of the earlier protesters might have joined the crowd, I thought it was a safe, but interesting topic; I'd used it previously for a press article. It combined a wide variety of sources, including private pornography of the late nineteenth century, a dramatic extract from the twenties bestseller, *The Sheik*, a wickedly amusing poem about homosexuality in the navy during the Second World War, and an unintentionally ludicrous scene from a recent popular novel. I put each extract in perspective with a brief discussion of the social background, the author's purpose and the expectations of the audience, then sank into a chair behind a table, ready to sign my book for anyone prepared to purchase it. Hugh had already warned me, "Don't sign until they own it." When I'd asked if I had to check receipts, he'd been irritated. "You know what I mean," he said, frowning at my frivolity.

Now he was beckoning me back to the lectern. "Answer questions," he said out of the corner of his mouth.

The first one was from small mousy woman who clutched a copy of *The Erotic Muse* as though she thought it might flutter away if given the chance. "There's an awful lot of sex in your book," she said briskly. "I want to know why."

"Well, it *is* on the subject of eroticism in literature . . ."

"On what?"

I was starting to lose confidence. "Eroticism?" I said hopefully, aware that Reyne was grinning widely at my discomfiture.

"There's another question at the back," interposed Hugh. This one was from an earnest young man who'd apparently learned by heart a convoluted question of interminable length. I followed a rule taught to me by one of my university teachers long ago — "The longer the question, the shorter the answer. That discourages them."

I was accustomed to questioning from my students, but this was a new experience. When someone asked how long I took to write the book, so many people nodded with approval that I realized this must be an important query, though why that should be I couldn't imagine.

Signing was another steep learning curve. A line snaked away from the table, each person holding at least one copy of the book — some, amazingly, several. Hugh was expert at shuffling on the ones who were determined to linger, leaving me to wrestle with the unlikely spellings that perfectly ordinary names seemed to have. I was reminded of the story about the visiting British author who'd dedicated a book to "Emma Chisit" only to find the customer was actually asking how much the book was.

At one point I looked up to see that Christie O'Keefe had arrived and was fiddling with an elaborate camera. I hated being photographed at the best of times, but felt doubly at a disadvantage when I was concentrating on inscribing suitable messages for those for whom a signature was not enough — "I'd like a few words, if you don't mind . . ."

The line eventually grew shorter, dwindling to a few determined people, one a large man with bulging eyes who confided that *he* was writing a book on erotica. As I declined his offer of co-authorship, and he reluctantly obeyed Hugh's admonitions that the appearance was over, Reyne came up behind me. "I enjoyed that. You had them eating out of your hand."

I'd expected a smart remark, but she seemed sincere. "Thank you."

"Christie and I are meeting in the Strand Arcade coffee shop. Want to join us?"

"I'm not sure . . ."

"The invitation's open. We'll be there for the next half hour at least." She nodded to Hugh, who was looking pleased with himself. "It went well," she said to him, "and I saw Pippa Blaine herself had turned up, rather than send a cub reporter."

He rubbed his hands. "Pippa Blaine . . ." In explanation, he said to me, "Pippa writes the Lifestyle column in the *Courier*. It's great press coverage and if we're lucky, she'll tie it in with a photo."

"Paul Chantrey spent of lot of time charming her."

Hugh groaned at Reyne's comment. "He'll be pushing publicity for his bookstore, not for Victoria. I'd better call Pippa and make sure she's got the right story."

"Feed her some juicy gossip and Pip will give you all the publicity you want," said Reyne with a mocking smile. She touched me lightly on the shoulder. "Coffee — if you want it . . ."

Watching her walk away, Hugh said, "I suppose you know . . ." He looked at me sideways. "No doubt someone's told you . . ."

"Told me what?"

"It's not a secret. She's quite open about it." He

dropped his voice to a conspiratorial level. "Reyne's gay . . . she's a lesbian."

"Really?"

I could hardly have conveyed less interest, but Hugh was determined to continue. "And I understand Christie's AC:DC — you know, both ways." When I didn't respond, he added, "Thought you should be told."

"Why?"

He was puzzled "Why? So you can . . ." He turned his palms up to indicate his point was self-evident.

"It's nothing to do with me, Hugh."

I could see he'd managed to embarrass himself. His color high, he blustered, "Now, how about that drink to celebrate your very successful appearance? The Hilton's just up the street and you might also like to look at where the literary luncheon is being held."

I gathered up my things. "Thanks, but I have to get back to the university."

As I made my way through the store, Hugh at my heels like an anxious-to-please Labrador dog, I overheard someone say, "See her? She's the professor who wrote that dirty book."

"Public recognition!" said Hugh. "Doesn't matter what they say, Victoria, as long as they say *something*."

The coffee shop was crowded, but Reyne and Christie had the best table near the window, where the constant movement of people walking through the restored Victorian shopping arcade provided a fascinating background. Looking at their casual clothing, I felt overdressed in my severely cut dark suit.

"Hey," said Christie, smiling broadly, "how's it feel to be a star?"

I eased myself into the chair crammed against the wall. "It has its downside. I just overheard a woman announce I'd written a dirty book."

"Perceptive comment," said Christie. "You have. That's why it's so successful."

Reyne was half-smiling, but also watching me closely. I wasn't used to being analyzed, assessed, so I challenged her. "There's something you want to say?"

"Just that you've got a great public persona."

Christie nodded. "You sure have, though I'm not sure how you do it."

I shrugged. "I'm used to lecturing . . ."

"Don't sell yourself short. It's a lot more than that. What do you think, Reyne?"

Uncomfortable under Reyne's analytical gaze, I was relieved when the coffee arrived. She stirred hers slowly, still considering me. "I think," she said, "Victoria manages to give the impression that under her uptight academic exterior there's a passionate woman."

"Under the uptight academic exterior," I said, my voice sharper than I intended, "is an uptight academic interior."

Her smile was knowing. "Hugh will assure you that it doesn't matter what you are — it's what you appear to be."

Touched by a vibration of anger, I said, "I'm

sure, Reyne, that you're *exactly* what you appear to be."

Christie chuckled. "Reyne's problem is she's short on hypocrisy and long on curiosity. She always wants to know what makes people tick."

Hugh's confidential tones came back to me. I absently stirred my coffee. *Lesbian,* I thought, turning the concept over in my mind. It was a mysterious word — not in its practical meaning, I understood that well enough — but in the resonances it had for me. In *The Erotic Muse* I'd included a wide range of homosexual references, including an exploration of the elaborate private codes used by serious writers to disguise homoeroticism.

If my Aunt Felice had lived to see the publication of my book, I knew she would have been sickened by any reference to homosexuality. I had vivid memories of cold Sunday evenings in winter, sitting chilled in the family pew with my aunt and cousins, while Uncle David in the pulpit loomed over me, his voice swooping and rising in denunciation of the sins of the flesh. Back then, he was a terrifying figure — not the forgetful, pathetic creature of the present, who shuffled to clutch my hand when I visited. All those evenings had coalesced into one recollection: my uncle, holding a Bible aloft, saliva spraying at his most impassioned moments, as he harangued his respectful congregation with powerful images of the sinful behavior that would earn God's most dreadful punishments. After one particularly vehement sermon, I asked Aunt Felice about a word I hadn't understood. Looking back, it was clear that my uncle's Sodom and Gomorrah theme that night had included female homosexuality. So many years later I could still feel the sting of my aunt's slap across my face, and her hissed command, "Don't you ever say that dirty, disgusting word again!"

I looked up to meet Reyne's cool appraisal. She said, "I need a preliminary interview with you as soon as possible. The whole scope of the article's been extended." My chin went up at her blunt tone, but she continued as though assured of my full cooperation. "*Millennium's* editorial board wants a full exploration of eroticism versus pornography in Western society — a series to cover literature, press, film, video — the lot. I've been assigned to coordinate literature and will be getting input from our international bureaus, but I think I should tell you I intend to make my article on *you* the focal point of the section."

Somewhat bemused by my elevation from author to focal point, I said, "I imagine I should be honored, but I can't quite see why you've chosen me."

Before Reyne could answer, Christie said, "We were discussing it before you joined us. *I* think it's a great idea because no one expects a professor of English to legitimize sexy writing the way you do." She glanced at Reyne. "But my friend here thinks the selling point is that you're an enigma — and everyone loves a mystery."

"I hope," said Reyne with a grin, "that you've got lots to hide, Victoria. I'd just hate it if you were superficial." Her smile widened. "But don't worry — if you're too boring, I'll make something up."

When I escaped to my familiar office, two

messages were waiting on my desk. One was from Gerald. I glanced at his neat request to see me, then frowned over the other message. It was from Zoe's brother, my cousin John, saying that Hugh Oliver had got him a ticket for my literary luncheon. As I was picking up the phone, Gerald came to the door.

"Victoria? About last night — I'm sorry for what happened."

I made a forget-it gesture, hoping that he'd be discouraged from a post mortem, but he came into the room, shutting the door behind him. "I think we need to talk."

It was the last thing I wanted to do. Looking at his thin, intense face, I was torn between blunt truth and some response that would maintain the friendship I valued. It was all too complicated, so I decided to stall. "It isn't a good time now."

He was persistent. "Then when? Tonight?" He smiled grimly at my expression. "Pushing you, am I?"

"It feels that way."

He nodded slowly. "Okay, let's give it a rest for a couple of days."

After he'd gone I swung my chair around and stared morosely out at the undergraduates strewn across the lawn like untidy drifts of leaves. Bursts of laughter and conversation floated through my open window and I was abruptly envious of youth and freedom. I was set in my ways, my life mapped out before me. I knew, with a heavy certainty, that I would spend it alone.

Gerald wasn't going to be easily deflected from the subject of a permanent relationship. I recoiled from even the idea, though he was the one man whom I could imagine tolerating physically for any length of time.

Bleakly, I considered my suitability for marriage, deciding that on a scale of one to ten, I was a minus. It was possible to tick off the points: I was too set in my ways; too independent; too self-sufficient . . . too detached.

Usually I liked to face things head on, but it was strange how unwilling I was to think about my frigidity. My thoughts always skittered away from the topic before it could disturb me too much. I didn't shrink from physical contact, it was just that it literally left me cold. I'd made a half-hearted attempt to discover why this dimension should be missing in me, but there were no answers, only questions. I didn't believe I'd ever been sexually abused — certainly I had no memory of anything like that — but my upbringing with my aunt and uncle had been strict and any show of affection was discouraged. Even so, John and Zoe had shared that same childhood, and neither appeared to have my remoteness of nature. It always came back to the same thing — it was *me*. There was something wrong with *me*.

It wasn't as if I'd kept myself aloof, virginal. I accepted with resignation the physical side of relationships, taking with bitter amusement Queen Victoria's reputed advice for women enduring the marital bed: "Look at the ceiling and think of England."

Of the men I'd known, Gerald had been the best, the most companionable of lovers, and I'd tolerated the sex because of friendship and shared interests. In bed he was painstaking and considerate, never demanding from me sensual abandonment. Wanting to please him, yet despising myself, I'd mimicked some response to his efforts, but it was a charade I knew I couldn't consider for any length of time, even though I enjoyed the illusion of closeness I gained from lying next to his body. At best I'd felt some slight physical arousal, but it was only in occasional dreams that I gained even a hint of what raw passion might be like — the scope of fulfillment physical delight might bring.

Picking up a copy of *The Erotic Muse,* I hefted it in my hand. This was what it came down to — passion captured in words. I could write about it — or rather, analyze the work of others who tried to capture the incandescence of love — but I had no reason to believe I would ever experience it myself, except at one remove.

CHAPTER THREE

"Actually," said the interviewer with a smug smile, "I haven't read your book yet." In case I should respond negatively, he hastily added, "But I intend to, as soon as possible."

I shifted my bulky earphones to a more comfortable position, glanced around the radio studio, then stared at the microphone that waited to suck up any entertaining words I might produce. I'd slept badly, so my second early morning radio interview was not something about which I could raise much enthusiasm.

The song that had been throbbing in my ears came to an end, the interviewer, unkempt, hairy and self-satisfied, smiled at me as he boomed, "And rise and shine, listeners! It's seven-thirty-five on a beautiful Sydney day, and with me in the studio I have the author of one of the hottest books around. And I mean hot! I've read it, and it *sizzles!*" If possible, he looked even more pleased with himself as he said, "Welcome, Professor Victoria Woodson, mega-selling writer of *The Erotic Muse!*"

Earlier, at the first radio station of the day, the questions had been reasonably thoughtful, including one that I had often wondered about myself: "Professor, why do you think the general public has shown such interest in erotica with a literary basis, when there's so much in the marketplace already in magazines and popular fiction?"

My answer had included the idea that an individual's very human interest in erotica was acceptable and defensible to that person when associated with literature. Such concepts would be beyond the ken of the oaf who was at present leering at me. "What do you say, Prof, if I suggest that all you've done is take the dirty bits out of a lot of old books, get a catchy title, and you're away with a bestseller?"

"I'd be speechless," I said dryly.

"So that isn't what you did?"

Some days before, a member of Hugh's publicity department had sat down with me to go through all the possible questions that might come up during media interviews. Fortified by this preparation, I launched on my "love and affection are the mainsprings of human experience" answer, and was

35

rewarded with a glazed expression from the other side of the console.

Leila Haven from Rampion's publicity department was accompanying me to each of the interviews, and as we walked to the carpark she remarked, "Thinks he's God, doesn't he? Comes from being one of the highest rated breakfast announcers around." Catching my expression, she added, "I know it's a drag doing interviews, but they sell books, believe me."

"I believe you. I just wonder if it's worth it."

"Gosh, yes," said Leila. "It pays my salary."

I'd agreed to a short preliminary interview with Reyne Kendall before I had to leave for the literary luncheon at the Hilton Hotel. Hugh had congratulated me on the number of people willing to pay to hear me speak — "It'll be packed! One of our most successful ever! And everyone'll have something to ask." Alerted by my experience of unexpected questions from the public at Chantrey's, I hoped to be ready for even the most extraordinary query that might be lobbed at me.

But I didn't feel well prepared for Reyne's questions. I'd only been back from the last radio interview for a short time when she knocked at the door. Dressed in casual pants, shirt and Reeboks, she filled my cramped room with confidence and energy — and I responded with hidden, baffled enmity. "Reyne, I'd like to know the direction your article's going to take . . . the scope, if you like."

She sat back to consider me. "I don't know yet." Her smile was surprisingly sweet. "It depends on you. I hate to admit it, but a lot of what I do just happens. Afterwards I'm more than happy to agree with anyone who comments on the structure and purpose, but while I'm writing it, frankly, I've got no idea what I'm doing."

I didn't really believe her, but nodded. She took a miniature tape recorder out of her bag and positioned it on my desk. "Do you mind me recording this?"

I shook my head, amused with the idea that possibly nods and shakes were the safest responses I could give to this vaguely threatening woman.

Reyne started off with a few brisk questions about my life and career. I passed a folder across my desk. "It's all in here — my degrees, publications . . ."

She grinned. "And do you list *The Erotic Muse* under academic publications?" Not leaving time for a response, she abruptly changed direction. "Tell me some general things about yourself."

"I'm not sure what you mean."

"Likes, dislikes, favorite things. How you spend your time. What you believe in, passionately."

This was turning into just the sort of interview I dreaded. "I can't quite see . . ."

"Oh, come on, Victoria. Humor me. Just do a bit of the stream-of-consciousness stuff."

"I'm no Virginia Woolf," I said lightly.

Her response was serious. "No, you're not, but what you are I don't yet understand."

Irritation was beginning to itch me. "Look, Reyne, I'm happy to talk about my work, my career, about this book. I don't see that anything else is relevant."

She smiled at me again, and, in spite of myself, it warmed me. "If I say *please* very persuasively?"

So I talked, careful always to run everything past an internal censor, but confident that I was providing a convincing picture of someone who could have been me. I felt safest discussing the academic world, but this concentration eventually seemed to irk Reyne. "Bit ivory-towerish, isn't it?" she said dismissively.

Exasperated, I said, "You think we're too cloistered, here at the university?"

"Well, if you ask me directly, yes." She shrugged. "Out here in the real world, you academics seem out of touch. I mean, you talk about things, you write about things. You never *do* them."

In my case, this was too close to home. Checking my watch, I said with a modicum of polite regret, "I'm sorry, we're out of time. I do have a luncheon . . ."

Reyne knew she'd hit home, but whether the strike was deliberate or not I didn't know. As she picked up her things she said, "Are you taking your car, or can I give you a lift? I'm going back into the city."

She was disturbing my ordered world, stirring up thoughts I didn't want to remember, but I hated to see myself as a coward. "Thank you," I said. "I'd appreciate it if you could drop me at the Hilton."

"I'd never drop you," said Reyne disconcertingly. "Trust me to always put you down gently."

* * * * *

The Hilton had hosted a multitude of literary lunches, most for luminaries far brighter than the author of a book on eroticism. I sat at the main table with Hugh and a selection of Rampion executives, eating an excellent lunch that I couldn't taste, conscious of the curious glances and whispered comments from surrounding tables. It was unusual for me to feel so nervous before speaking. I glanced surreptitiously at my notes. I'd decided on a smorgasbord of readings, tied together by the general heading of my talk: *The Infinite Variety of Love.* I intended to show that erotica, irrespective of whether society condoned or condemned, ran as a constant counterpoint to popular and literary writing, and that both heterosexual and homosexual love were celebrated in ways that often offended, but also intrigued, the society of the time.

"Think I should warn you," said Hugh, "that there are some religious heavies from the establishment here today." He beamed at me. "Be as controversial as you like, Victoria." His advice was sales-centered: one of the reasons *The Erotic Muse* had gained so much censure was because I'd included extensive erotic writings from religious references — not only from the writings of supposed celibates and moral leaders, but quotations from publications where Church money or influence had been the means of support and distribution of the literary product. I'd scrupulously checked and documented my references, but this hadn't stopped the almost hysterical indignation of the established religious bodies and many of their followers.

While I was covertly surveying the room to see if I could detect familiar opponents, my cousin John came up to give me a light embrace. "Proud of you, Vicky," he said. He was the only person who shortened my name, and I'd never been able to break him of the habit. Strangely, his presence, which during my childhood had been a comfort, today only made me more anxious. He went back to his table some distance from the official party, and as I went up to the raised lectern I looked for his square, serious face.

My audience, soothed by good food and wine, waited indulgently for me to begin. My introductory remarks described my experiences as the original scholarly work was transformed into a much racier study on literary erotica. Buoyed by appreciative laughter, I explained some of the editing suggestions, including chapter headings that had both amused and bemused me — my favorite being my editor's firm conviction — one I resisted — that the section exploring erotic poetry should be called *Lusty Lyrics*.

After I read selected passages, I fielded my first question from an angular man with a flamboyant bow tie. "The subject seems to me to be a very strange choice for a lady of your undoubted stature in the academic world."

I'd been asked this before, and gave the suitably erudite reply that, so far, had satisfied my interrogators. It didn't, however, answer my own queries. I knew that I delighted in the subject of love and passion, at least when it was safely caught in words, not actions. My response was an intellectual one, not physical, and it only took a touch of amateur psychology for me to accept that I had substituted fiction for reality. Perhaps I was suppressing a wild sexuality, but somehow I doubted it.

A tall, well-dressed woman smiled at me broadly, then asked in bold, ringing tones if I found my work on erotica titillating. *"I* would," she added, looking around as if expecting her statement to be challenged. "Think I'd be in a constant state of arousal!"

She hadn't really wanted me to reply — just an opportunity to make a mildly outrageous comment. As if to show her the standard expected at a literary luncheon, the next question — from an intense young man — contained so many references to obscure writers that I became lost in its convolutions, and so gave a answer that sent the questioner back to his seat with a puzzled frown.

Inevitably, someone wanted to know how long it took to write the book. I responded on automatic pilot, while I wondered why Reyne hadn't asked me directly why I'd written *The Erotic Muse.* I didn't like the possibilities, particularly the thought that she might assume that I somehow got an unhealthy sexual fillip from the subject.

"Professor Woodson? I have an important question." The man's tone was already ringing with righteousness. Recognizing his fleshy, arrogant face, I sighed. Brilliant at working the media, he was a fundamentalist in every sense of the word. His savage campaigns against women who aspired to be anything other than subsidiary to men were legendary — and in me he had a double target. Not only was I female and a professor, I had also written something he considered to be the work of the devil. He looked around to make sure everyone was attentive before continuing, "Was it only crass commercialism that drove you to attack the Church, and those who serve her faithfully, or did you have some other, even more reprehensible, motive?"

I said firmly, "Surely it's clear from even a casual reading of my work that I had no intention of attacking anyone, or, indeed, any institution such as the Church. What I set out to do was to trace the history of a particular strand of literature."

"Literature!" He spat the word. "By any standard this filth is not literature. And these lies, these fabrications about men who have devoted their lives to God . . . pure evil!"

"I did include female religious," I said mildly.

He ignored my comment. "It can only undermine the foundations of society when the family, the Church, the moral fiber . . ."

I tuned out his familiar phrases. Glancing at the official table I saw that Hugh had a half-smile — the more outrageous the controversy, the better the publicity.

Silence alerted me that my reply was due. In contrast to my questioner's loud outrage, I spoke with tones of reason and persuasion, pointing out that the existence of such material was well documented, that erotica had existed throughout social history, and that I had merely recorded and commented upon certain writings, including some that had a religious background.

My moderate reply generated a few more spluttering condemnations, then a comment from someone obviously impatient with the slant sent the questioning in a different direction. Finally, Hugh whisked me away to a table for the publisher's reward — a book signing. I was becoming more skilled at putting a bland comment and then signing my name, smiling, and then rapidly moving to the next person in line.

John waited until the last lingering person had been dispatched by Hugh, then gave me a hug. "That was great, Vicky, great. I feel really proud to know you."

"I don't think Zoe is."

"Oh, Zoe . . ." My cousin smiled indulgently. "You know what she's like. Underneath it all she admires you. She just can't say it."

Unconvinced, I managed a neutral murmur that could have indicated agreement.

As we went down to the hotel carpark, he said, "Saw that journalist who's doing your story."

"What, on TV?"

He stopped walking and turned to me. "I got the impression you knew all about it. She didn't actually say, but —"

"Reyne Kendall's *interviewed* you? In person?"

"Yes. Quite early this morning. She wanted some background, she said. I didn't see it as a problem . . ." His voice trailed off at my expression.

I wished my words were bullets I could fire. "How dare she do that."

John hated conflict, so he tried to placate me. "Hang on, Vicky. There were no really personal questions. I wouldn't have answered them if there had been. I just gave her some general information she could have got from other sources anyway."

Ridiculously, I felt betrayed. "I suppose it'll be Zoe, next," I said with some bitterness.

John's face showed guilty amusement. "I hate to say this, but Reyne Kendall's seeing Zoe about now, actually."

I turned my anger inward, as I had from the time I was a child. "I hope Zoe keeps at least in sight of the truth," I said with a rueful smile.

John, who never seemed able to see beneath the surface, relaxed at this indication of a reasonable attitude. "Of course she will — and anyway, as far as Zoe's concerned, I got the idea Reyne Kendall's more interested in photos and stuff like that."

I could hear the undercurrent of resentment in my voice as I said, "I don't see what my childhood's got to do with the book."

John put an arm around my shoulders. "You just have to accept it," he said mockingly. "You're a star, Victoria Woodson. It must be hell."

Although feeling positively murderous towards Reyne, I matched his flippant tone. "It *is* hell," I said, "but it's my academic duty to endure it."

He kissed my cheek. "Bye, Vicky. See you tomorrow night."

"Tomorrow night?"

"Zoe hasn't checked with you yet? Well, that's fairly typical. I bet you find a message on your answering machine summoning you. She's already asked Gerald, and I'm going. Come on, Vicky, don't frown. We don't see enough of you, as it is, so don't say you can't make it."

John's wife had died a year ago, and though I'd spent time with him in the first few months, I was uneasily aware that I'd neglected him recently. "All right," I said, "but only if you protect me from Zoe when she launches into an attack on my book."

His pleasure at my acceptance made me feel guilty. "Haven't I always protected you?" he said. "Particularly from Zoe?"

Reyne answered at the third ring. "Reyne Kendall."

Now that I had her on the phone, I wasn't quite sure what to say. The righteous indignation of, "How dare you talk to my family," would sound absurd, if not paranoid. I said, my voice chilly, "I was a little surprised you didn't mention that you were seeing my cousins for background."

"That was deliberate," said Reyne. "It's my policy not to warn people that I'm going to see their relatives."

I glared at the phone as though it were Reyne. "Why?" I snapped.

"To stop the problem of rehearsing and editing memories. People often like to polish up the past."

"I can't imagine I'd go to the trouble."

"It's not personal — it's just my policy."

Keeping my voice even, I said, "Were John and Zoe helpful?"

Reyne's warm chuckle ran down the line and curled into my ear. "If you mean am I any closer to understanding you, Professor, the answer's no." She paused for my response. When I remained silent, she added, "But I can assure you I'm enjoying the search."

CHAPTER FOUR

Warmth spiraled through me. The lover who held me in a tight embrace ran a tongue along my closed lips. I opened my mouth to the pressure. The pulse of my desire made me gasp. "Please," I groaned...

The alarm shrilled, jolting me awake. I kept my eyes squeezed shut, but the dream evaporated, leaving only a wisp of passion to taunt me. Reluctantly I blinked in the early morning brightness of my orderly bedroom. There was something about the day I didn't like... then I remembered the midday appointment to appear live on Chisholm Tierce's television show.

Tao, who had been galvanized into action by the alarm, continued to complain bitterly about imminent starvation as I slid out of bed, straightened the sheets that I'd churned into a twisted mess, and padded into the bathroom. My reflection stared back at me, the same controlled, quietly watchful face as always. I wondered what I would look like in the abandonment of lovemaking — not the sedate coupling that Gerald and I indulged in, but the wild, uninhibited passion that I dimly remembered from my dream.

I arrived early at the television studio — running late always causes me such anxiety that I overcompensate — to find Hugh Oliver already there. Carrying two mugs of coffee, he followed me into the makeup room. As the grim young woman in a bright pink smock surveyed me critically before making a selection from her impressive array of bottles and tubes, I said to him, "Waiting to see meek professor transformed into effervescent television personality?"

Even under the harsh lighting his skin glowed with ruddy health. "Not so meek," he said, handing me one of the coffees, which was prepared just as I always had it — black with one sugar. Hugh prided himself on his ability to remember likes, dislikes and preferences. "Always impresses people," he'd confided shortly after I met him. He had laughed when I'd pointed out that telling me of his achievement somewhat lessened the impact. "Not so," he'd said.

"Now you think you're being treated differently because I'm letting you in on professional secrets."

Both Hugh and I watched in the mirror as the makeup woman went to work, turning my pale reflection into an exaggerated version of myself. As I looked doubtfully at her handiwork, she said tersely, "It'll look all right on the screen. The lights wash you out, you see."

As she spoke, Christie O'Keefe came into the room. "You're early, Victoria. I'm on before you."

"I didn't realize you'd be here too."

She raised a satiric eyebrow. "I suspect Hugh and my magazine got together to arrange it."

Hugh bestowed his usual sunny smile. "And you'll mention Victoria and your photographs for *Millennium*, won't you?"

Christie grinned. "You sure have chutzpah, Hughie. Chisholm Tierce is interviewing me about *my* career. Anyway, Victoria's quite capable of beating her own drum."

Hugh spread his hands. "Every little bit helps."

While he went off to check that things were going to schedule, I stayed chatting to Christie while her makeup was applied. "I hear you had a run-in with Reyne," she said.

"Not exactly. She saw my cousins without telling me, and I suppose I resented it." As I spoke, I realized that it must sound like an overreaction, so I added, "I'm a private person. I don't like my family being asked questions."

I'd amused Christie. "Honey," she said, "you've gotten yourself into the wrong business. You get fame — you get questions. Goes with the territory."

"You're done," said the makeup woman, who had

altered Christie's lightly tanned face into a distinct brown contrast with her pale blonde hair.

As we went down the corridor towards the studio, I said casually, "What did Reyne say?"

"Not much. Just that you were quite an interesting challenge."

"I'm unhappy to hear I'm only *quite* interesting," I said lightly, wondering why I was curious about what Reyne might, or might not, have said.

A young man with a clipboard and a harassed expression hurried up to us. "Christie O'Keefe? Professor Woodson? You're needed now." He clucked over his list. "The running order's shot to pieces," he declared. Shoving open a heavy metal door he gestured urgently. "Through here, please."

The studio was unremittingly ugly. Uncomfortable-looking plastic chairs rose in tiers for the members of the audience, who were already filing into their seats, even though the show wasn't due to start for some time. Looking down on us from one wall was the lit window of the control room. People hastened by, each preoccupied with some mysterious task. Thick cables snaked over the grubby concrete floor, and banks of lights hung from a jumble of metal framework suspended from the ceiling. The cameras sat like wheeled alien monsters, each with a human attendant wearing earphones and the worn blue jeans which seemed to be the uniform required for the crew. The familiar set of *The Chisholm Tierce Show* — even I had succumbed to the extravagant plaudits and had watched it once or twice — looked unconvincingly flimsy in the brilliant flat light that bathed its tacky outlines. Glancing at a monitor, I was surprised at how the camera made the set look substantial and attractive. I pointed out the screen to Christie. "The camera makes the set look good. Can it do that for us?"

She wrinkled her nose. "You, maybe. Me? I'd need a couple more hours in makeup."

I smiled at her agreeable face, thinking how easy she was to be with — by contrast to Reyne's company.

Chisholm Tierce, his sleek good looks enhanced by the heavy television makeup, came over to gladhand us. "Ladies! Wonderful to have you here with us. We've got a great show today . . ." He beckoned to the worried young man with the clipboard. "Barry? Over here." Turning his smooth charm on us again, he said, "Barry will show you the ropes, make sure you feel comfortable." He looked past us to where another guest — a well-known plastic surgeon — had entered the studio. "Excuse me." As he swept towards the new arrival, his rich tones floated back to us. "Dr. Enrico! Wonderful to have you here with us. We've got a great show today . . ."

"Lucky we hit him on an up day," said Christie dryly.

Hugh joined us as Barry began instructions on the procedures to be followed and the dos and don'ts of guest appearances. He pointed out the floor manager, who was standing with arms folded waiting for Tierce's attention. "He's in charge of what happens down here, while the director in the control room decides what actually goes to air." Christie was obviously an old hand at all this, but I was becoming almost as anxious as Hugh looked. *The Chisholm Tierce Show* was broadcast live at noon, so if I made some embarrassing mistake it couldn't be edited out, but would be seen by the whole huge audience.

"Don't worry," said Hugh. "It'll be a breeze."

Christie's smile was mischievous. "Sure Chisholm's been briefed properly, Hugh? You wouldn't want him asking any questions out of left field . . ." Her smile broadened as he excused himself and hurried away. "He's so easy to panic it takes all the fun out of it."

The atmosphere was taking an air of urgency as the time ticked towards noon. The guests for the show — me, Christie, Dr. Enrico and a well-known astrologer who'd had the skill, or luck, to predict several major world disasters — were shepherded into a waiting area. An exhaustingly energetic woman in a red jacket appeared on stage to warm up the audience. Within a few minutes she had turned a crowd of individuals into a good-humored, cohesive group who laughed and applauded enthusiastically when instructed by flashing red signs. A few minutes before midday Chisholm Tierce entered to a positive storm of adulation from his largely middle-aged, female audience.

The apparent chaos of the studio was contradicted by the smooth running of the show once the well-known theme was played. It was fascinating to glance from the monitor, where everything was the familiar seamless production, to the swooping cameras and the jumble of equipment just out of view of the lens.

Barry stood with us like a sheepdog whose flock might wander. He checked his clipboard, assuring us yet again that the running order of guests was Dr.

Enrico first, followed by Christie, then me. The astrologer had the final spot, and from Barry's nervous questions, I gathered that some extraordinary prediction was to be made as the show closed. Hugh was with the director, and he waved from the control room above us, his face reflecting poorly disguised stress.

The mosaic of the program emerged, as banter from Tierce was followed by a singer, advertisements, the first interview, more banter, a news flash, more ads, then Christie. I watched in admiration, sure that I wouldn't be able to imitate her cheerful insouciance as she chatted animatedly, ignoring the cameras crowding the one brightly lit area of the studio. She told amusing anecdotes from her travels as a photographer, and I found myself laughing along with the audience.

My amusement died as Barry whispered, "You're next, Professor. When I give the signal, get onto the set, sit down, and be ready to go."

Why had I thought a book-signing or a literary luncheon challenging? This was much more daunting. Tierce turned a big smile to the camera, then an advertisement for mouthwash appeared on the monitor. Barry tapped my shoulder. Someone had dashed in to dab at Tierce's brow. I stumbled past Christie on her way off the set. "Give 'em hell," she said with a grin. I didn't smile in return, being too busy negotiating the obstacle course of equipment and cables. The heat of the lights hit my face as I lowered myself into the chair, my mind completely blank. I hadn't felt this intensity of stagefright for years, not since my first public lecture. Chisholm Tierce was snarling at the floor manager. I stared at a monitor, where a white-coated man was sincerely extolling the virtues of an antacid powder. The floor manager stepped away from the set, holding up his fingers to indicate seconds elapsing. The ad ended, the logo of the program appeared — I was on camera.

Tierce's annoyance had disappeared a moment before his image appeared on the screen. Now he looked playful, almost boyish, as he remarked upon the controversy *The Erotic Muse* had generated. The studio audience murmured, though whether in approval or disapproval I couldn't tell. As he introduced me with a few brief comments, I found myself staring fixedly at the camera, quite mesmerized by its single intrusive eye. I'd been given an outline of the innocuous questions likely to be asked, but Chisholm Tierce didn't stick to the script. "Are you obsessed with sex?" he asked cheerily.

I heard my voice as if from a distance, and was comforted at its normality. I even managed a lilting laugh. "Obsessed with sex? I don't believe so."

"Then why this particular book, Professor Woodson?" He shot a sly smile to the studio audience as he held a copy for the camera to focus upon. "I'd imagine you'd have to wade through an awful lot of sexy material just doing the research . . ." As he paused, someone in the audience tittered. He gave a roguish smile as he continued, "And, Professor, some of it must have needed quite some searching to find — the scandalous religious writings, for instance."

Before I could explain that the erotica was written by people in the Church, but wasn't religious by any definition, he had gone on to say, "I believe your book has been denounced from the pulpits of several denominations. I'm sure my audience would like to know your personal religious background and beliefs."

I began to feel more comfortable with what was becoming a familiar query. Almost forgetting the venue, I concentrated on Tierce's face. After all, posing and answering questions were aspects of my profession, so there was no reason to be rattled. The time passed so quickly that it seemed only a few moments and then my interview was expertly wound up with yet another knowing smile from Chisholm Tierce.

Hugh came to meet me as I made my way back through the maze of cameras and cables. "Excellent, Victoria! That should sell a few books. I've asked for a copy of the tape, so you can review how it went."

"I don't think I want to see it."

Christie gave me a companionable squeeze. "If you change your mind," she said, "I know Reyne's taped it."

"Whatever for?"

"You'll learn," said Christie, "that when Reyne Kendall does a story, she really researches it."

I nodded, thinking irritably that Reyne was intruding far too much into my life.

Zoe was in full hostess mode. She was an excellent cook and specialized in elaborate dishes which generally tasted as good as they looked. Tonight, however, she'd prepared a dish featuring quail, and their tiny, pathetic bodies, however artistically arranged, stirred a latent vegetarianism in me. I seemed to be the only one so affected. John was crunching fragile bones with enthusiasm and Gerald had already consumed the little corpses on his plate. Arthur, Zoe's husband, dabbed at his neat mustache with his napkin. "Excellent, darling," he said to Zoe.

I didn't join the appreciative noises, being fully occupied arranging the contents of my plate so it would appear I'd made a decent attempt at eating the little quail remains.

"So, Victoria," said Arthur a little too heartily, "you're getting to be quite famous."

I opted for a modest expression as Zoe sniffed disparagingly. "Notorious, more likely," she said.

Gerald smiled tentatively from the other side of the table. He hadn't offered to drive me here for dinner, but had turned up a little late — I, of course, had irked Zoe by being early — and had treated me with a careful camaraderie.

Before Gerald's arrival Zoe had made an unsuccessful cross-examination about our relationship, so I wasn't surprised when she smiled winningly and said, "Gerald, we really *must* see more of you and Victoria. Perhaps a weekend away in the Blue Mountains would be nice? What do you think?"

"Darling . . ." Arthur cleared his throat. "You know I'm in the middle of a new software project. I could have trouble taking time off at this point."

Zoe frowned. To rescue him, I said, "I'm afraid I've got appearances in Brisbane and Melbourne, and then the tour of the States . . ."

Her frown deepening, Zoe said to Gerald, "What do you think of it? This book Victoria's written?" Her tone made it obvious *she* didn't approve, and expected he would concur.

"I think *The Erotic Muse* is great. It's well written and researched, and introduces the general public to material that might not otherwise be accessible."

From Zoe's expression she was clearly disappointed in Gerald's answer. "That's all very well," she said, "but you have to count the cost to the family. Both John and I have been pestered by a journalist wanting information about Victoria. Kendall, her name is. Has she approached you?"

"She left a message. I haven't got back to her yet."

"You didn't tell me," I said sharply.

"I didn't have the opportunity."

Sensing potential conflict, Arthur looked vaguely alarmed. Gerald's face was blank. Zoe smiled. She always seemed to gain energy from arguments, either as a participant or an observer. "The Kendall woman asked me a lot of personal questions," she said smugly. "Of course, I did try to protect your privacy, Victoria."

"I can imagine . . ."

Zoe leaped into one of her abrupt rages. "*I* protect the family, at least! I don't go round writing unsavory books . . ."

I ignored the challenge, saying mildly, "What exactly did you tell Reyne Kendall?"

She shrugged. "What was there to tell? It's not as if any of us had an interesting childhood, is it?"

I thought, *For me it was sometimes frightening, and always emotionally sterile.* Aloud I said, "I suppose not."

There was a tinge of malice in Zoe's voice. "I did give her some photographs. Thought you wouldn't mind."

"I do mind."

Arthur said, "Just family snaps. That's all."

His attempt to humor me failed. "I'd have appreciated being asked permission first," I said coldly.

"She said she'd return them," said Zoe, perfectly aware that this wasn't the point I was making. She stood up. "Clear the plates, please Arthur. I'll get dessert."

I snatched the plates from Arthur and followed her into her gleaming, space-age kitchen. "Look, Zoe, you're always talking about family solidarity, so how about showing some over this?"

Zoe's anger had dissipated. "Victoria," she said indulgently, "I'll do anything I can . . . but of course, you've only got yourself to blame, haven't you?"

CHAPTER FIVE

Gerald insisted on driving me to the airport for the early morning flight to Brisbane. I was wary of encouraging him, although he hadn't taken the dinner at Zoe and Arthur's to mean that we were to resume our previous level of intimacy. He was now treating me as a dear friend, rather than a lover. I valued his comradeship and hoped, without much conviction, that he would abandon any idea of pursuing a deeper relationship.

After I'd checked my luggage, and we dawdled over cups of coffee and awkward conversation, Gerald embraced me briefly, said, "Have a good time," and left me at the entry gate.

I hadn't seen or heard from Reyne for several days, although I was aware that she'd contacted different colleagues and acquaintances because she'd sent me a fax at the university listing the names. There'd been a sarcastic little scrawl at the bottom: *For your information only.* At the time I'd been only mildly annoyed, so when I saw Reyne waiting to board the plane, I was surprised by the intensity of my anger. "Considerate of you to send me that fax, but surely you must have wondered if I'd get to them first."

Reyne grinned at me. "Did you?"

"Of course. I coached each and every one of them with laudatory things to say about me. Surely you noticed?"

She seemed amused at my sarcastic tone, but before she could reply we were interrupted by a breathless, "Thank God I've made it!" Hugh Oliver wasn't squiring me to Brisbane, but was sending Leila Haven from Rampion's publicity department to stand in for him. "Almost missed the plane," Leila added unnecessarily. She smiled at me as if sure I'd approve of her tardiness, then said to Reyne, "Hi! You coming with us too?"

"Yes, but not just for Rampion and Victoria — I'll be doing some work on a police corruption story as well."

Leila nodded wisely. "Yeah, good thing you've got something else, because there's not much in this for you . . . I mean, Brisbane's pretty much a hick town, so it doesn't really matter what Victoria does."

Reyne gave me a small smile. "I don't know. She might do something outrageous."

"I wouldn't hold my breath," I advised.

On the plane, Leila, who was always eager to talk, had the seat beside mine. Contemplating an hour of chatter put me in defense mode. "I have a great deal of marking to do," I said firmly, as I opened my briefcase and took out a bundle of students' papers. Soon I was concentrating deeply, only sighing now and then at the original spelling and grammar that some young people used.

I looked up with a prickle of irritation when Reyne leaned over to ask Leila to change seats with her, then went resolutely back to my marking. Reyne didn't speak, but I was conscious that she was watching me. I put down my pen. "Yes?"

"I don't mean to interrupt you . . ."

Refusing to make a polite rejoinder, I looked directly at her. "Is there something you want?"

Reyne looked solemn. "I think you might have taken that list of contact names I faxed to you as a sort of sarcastic comment."

"Wasn't that exactly what it was?"

A winning smile accompanied her reply. "I suppose you could read it that way . . . or you could accept that I was keeping you informed because you'd complained earlier I hadn't told you I was approaching your cousins."

Reyne brought out in me an unsuspected talent for confrontation. "Enlighten me," I said coldly. "Which particular motive was it?"

"To be truthful, both." She looked away from me, a flush under her fair skin. "It was unprofessional, but you got to me — I don't know why. What I'd like to do is apologize, and hope you'll forget it."

Her obvious sincerity surprised me. I recalled Christie's comments about Reyne being thrown by my being a professor, and was disarmed. My voice several degrees warmer, I said, "Anyone on the list come up with something absolutely scandalous about me?"

She correctly read this as a peace offering. "Not a thing," she said. "You've obviously led a blameless life."

Several times after I'd gone back to my marking, I glanced at her profile as she sat beside me. My initial dislike was now diluted with curiosity and a grudging respect. Reyne was obviously much more than the stereotypical journalist I had conceived her to be. The depth and feeling in her article on street children had told me that much. I recognized that at least some of the antipathy I felt was due to resentment that she had a free hand to delve into my life as though I were nothing more than one of her investigative projects.

My Brisbane schedule began with a lunchtime appearance and signing at a large city bookstore, a few press interviews during the afternoon, and then a dinner arranged by the State branch of Rampion Press to which a selection of local VIPs had been invited. The next day was to be devoted to covering morning radio programs, together with taping a segment for television.

The pace of life in Brisbane was noticeably

slower than in Sydney and my booksigning was correspondingly casual and low key. I almost looked for controversial questions, but along with the familiar, *How long did it take to write the book?* were innocuous queries about what time of day I wrote, whether I used a computer, and how I'd researched the material. It was as though everyone there was too well bred to mention sex, although I was astonished when the group applauded politely after I'd read an example of eroticism from the mid-Victorian era.

Leila, obviously delighted with the responsibility, spent the whole day rushing around, talking incessantly and mentioning at regular intervals that she was from Rampion's publicity department, as she pressed her business card into reluctant hands. She seemed to have taken a vow never to let me out of her sight, but when checking that everything was running smoothly for the evening function threw her into a frenzy of activity, my patience finally wore thin. I announced, to Leila's deep concern, an entirely fictitious headache and the need for a couple of quiet hours before the official dinner.

Alone in my suite — Rampion Press was sparing no expense — I kicked off my shoes and sank into the accommodating softness of a plump sofa. I wanted to regain the feeling that I was in control, that mine was the quiet center about which chaos and confusion might revolve, but never touch. Familiarity soothed me, and I longed for my own little house, or my spartan office at the university. Looking around the anonymous luxury of the suite, I tried to attain the inner stillness that I'd developed as a defense in childhood and which had helped me throughout my adult life. It included the ability to stand back, to be uninvolved, to feel apart and protected by that isolation.

I shut my eyes — and saw Reyne Kendall's face. She was an irritant that I couldn't dismiss from my mind. I'd no idea why she should have this disquieting effect, and was becoming increasingly impatient with my inability to banish her to where she belonged — a temporary factor on the periphery of my life.

Reyne had attended my lunchtime appearance, and had then disappeared. I didn't see her again until late that night after my VIP dinner, which had turned out to be much more enjoyable than I'd expected. I'd worn a new black dress and had my hair up in a fashion that, for me, was positively frivolous. Leila and I climbed out of our limousine at the hotel entrance just as Reyne was paying off a taxi. Leila hurried off — "Want to ring my boyfriend before he goes to sleep" — leaving me with Reyne, who immediately suggested a nightcap.

When I demurred, she said, "Join me. You look like you've had a good time, so why not finish it off with champagne?"

I didn't often drink champagne, but enjoyed the irresponsible sizzle of its bubbles. Besides, I'd had enough alcohol with dinner to make me feel pleasantly relaxed, so I found myself agreeing to Reyne's suggestion. She took my arm. "Let's miss the bar and call room service."

"All right. Your room or mine?"

"Has Rampion splurged and put you in a suite?"

"Yes."

Reyne's dimple appeared. "Then there isn't any choice."

We talked companionably on the way up to my suite. Wondering where she'd been — she was wearing a sophisticated outfit of black satin pants and top, and, for the first time since we'd met, noticeable makeup — I said, "You've been out on the town?"

"You might say that. Illegal casino, actually, but very up-market."

I was intrigued, having never knowingly done anything illegal in my life. "What if the casino had been raided, and you'd been arrested?"

"Unlikely," said Reyne with a grin. "I was gambling with some of the top cops in the state."

I was abruptly aware of how different her experience of life was from mine, and I felt a growing interest in what had made her the tough, uncompromising person she was.

When we reached my suite, I ordered champagne from room service, feeling vaguely wicked. While Reyne was prowling around like a cat checking out a new domain, there was a knock at the door. The waiter, who hardly looked old enough to be handling alcohol, looked disappointed when Reyne said she'd open the bottle. "You sure?" he said doubtfully as he put the tray on the table. "Champagne corks can be really tight."

"I'm sure, but I'll call you if I have any trouble."

She charged the order to her room — "It was my idea, Victoria" — swept the waiter out the door, and smiled at me. Like Zoe's smile, Reyne's was a potent weapon. But whereas Zoe's made me wary, Reyne's, in spite of my best efforts, charmed me.

Picking up the bottle, she said, "Now it's a matter of pride. I'll have to get this open, even if I'm forced to knock the top off in the bathroom." I noticed she was left-handed as she removed the wire cage, and with an expert twist, eased out the cork with a satisfying pop.

We sat opposite each other in comfortable lounge chairs separated by a low marble table. She raised her glass to me. "You look great."

I was pleased and embarrassed at the same time, so I covered up with a reciprocal compliment about her appearance.

Reyne chuckled. "Now that we've established we're both terrific, how about we get down to something important?"

"All right," I said. "What made you decide to be a journalist?"

"Decide? Perhaps I just fell into it."

I sipped my champagne, enjoying its clean astringency. "I don't believe you would just fall into anything."

She looked gratified, as though I'd given her a special commendation. Wanting, unaccountably, to know much more about her, I said, "Was anyone else in your family involved in journalism?"

"Hardly. I'm the success story, the one who made good." The lightness of her tone couldn't disguise a trace of bitterness. My interrogative expression made her smile wryly. "I come," she said, "from a family of what might politely be called underachievers. I don't think my Dad has held a job for more than a few months. He suffers, he always says, from *my bloody bad back,* but it's never stopped him from drinking, gambling . . . you name it. It's only work of any description that seems to cause the problem."

"You have brothers, sisters?"

She paused long enough for me to decide that she regretted giving me any personal information, but then she said freely, "Two brothers, one sister. Each of my brothers has done his best to emulate my father's lifestyle. They're on welfare most of the time, milk the system for what they can get . . ." She shook her head. "It's not that they're stupid, or even unpleasant — it's that my father's taught them well. He believes the world owes you a living, and you'd be a fool to bust your guts working."

I was surprised at her honesty and curious enough to want her to continue. "Your sister?"

Reyne stared at the bubbles in her glass. "She takes after my mother. Married a man just like Dad — a no-hoper. Mum has her church, her martyrdom, her beaten-down-isn't-life-cruel conversation." She glanced at me. "Sorry. I'm complaining just like Mum does."

Feeling an unexpected kinship with her, I said, "Your family's proud of you." I made it a statement, not a question, as if that way I could make it true.

"*Proud* isn't quite the word I'd use . . . *puzzled,* perhaps." She smiled without humor. "But they're all pleased I have a good income. I give cash for presents — birthdays, Christmas — and it's always appreciated."

There was a silence between us. Reyne looked down at her clenched right hand, I sought vainly for a response that wasn't just a platitude.

Abruptly, she said, "You haven't married."

Totally disconcerted, I snapped back, "Neither have you."

Reyne looked surprised. "Of course I haven't. I can't believe Hugh hasn't fallen over himself in his rush to tell you that I'm a lesbian."

"I'm sorry. I forgot."

"You *forgot?*"

I felt nettled by her tone. "Hugh did mention it at Chantrey's Bookstore . . . I suppose I didn't find it important." As I spoke, I realized I wasn't telling the truth. From the time Hugh had told me, the fact that Reyne was a lesbian had given a disturbing, almost exciting, edge to my thoughts about her.

Leaning over to refill my glass, Reyne smiled at me. "Forgive me. I'm very self-centered tonight. It's my birthday."

"Happy birthday," I said automatically, raising my champagne in a salute. The phrase had a sharp emotional charge for me. Aunt Felice and Uncle David had not believed in the celebration of birthdays, other than an acknowledgment that the day was an anniversary of one's birth. Presents, a party — these were unacceptable indulgences. The one concession I remembered was that on my birthday I was permitted to choose a favorite dinner, as long as it was good, plain food.

"At least," said Reyne, "my family does love an excuse for a party. Mum was very upset I'd be away today, even though with my job I'm often out of Sydney. She loves to get everyone celebrating someone's birthday, or Christmas, as though it will make us stay together as a family the rest of the time." She frowned reflectively. "But for as long as I can remember, I've felt in some way an outsider."

I felt a sudden rush of affinity for her. "When you were a child, did you always know there must be something better out there? That all you had to do was grow up and you'd be able to go out and find it?"

She nodded slowly. "But it wasn't what I expected."

I looked away, regretting that I'd let down my guard. My tone deliberately conversational, I said, "I don't suppose it ever is."

As if by unspoken agreement, we turned to less personal topics. We chatted like superficial friends who had never crossed the line into genuine closeness. Her dry sense of humor delighted me, as did the strength with which she held her convictions. I had always been drawn to people who not only felt things strongly, but knew *why* they did, and Reyne could argue her case with both sincerity and evidence to support it.

And running like a whisper under our conversation was my awareness of her homosexuality. I didn't question why it made any difference to me — I just knew that it did.

"I'd better go," she said. "You've got an early start tomorrow morning."

I saw her to the door, then, impelled by a sudden impulse, I kissed her lightly on the cheek. "Happy birthday, again."

Her quick smile stayed with me long after I'd closed the door.

CHAPTER SIX

When I returned to Sydney I made a duty visit that I dreaded, but could never allow myself to avoid. My cousin John had called and arranged for us to meet at the nursing home. He was waiting for me in the car park, even though I arrived a few minutes early. "Hi, Vicky," he said somberly, his substantial square frame looming over me. "Matron Scott called yesterday to say Dad's getting worse. Over the last few days he's been practically bedridden."

I looked at the facade of The Good Shepherd

retirement home and hospital with aversion. A graceless building painted a clinical white, its interior was as characterless as its exterior suggested. Uncle David being a minister, he was entitled to spend his declining years in the chilly comfort of this Church establishment. When his mind had started to deteriorate, Aunt Felice had shown little patience with the difficulties he caused, and had handed him over to The Good Shepherd's formidable matron with dispatch.

"It was hearing about Mum that did it," said John as we entered the antiseptic atmosphere. "I know we didn't think he understood when we told him that she'd died, but Matron Scott says at some level, he knew."

I didn't reply. There was nothing of comfort I could say, and I was fighting the familiar mixture of anger, repulsion and guilt that visiting my uncle always caused me. I wanted to feel sympathy, sorrow — I knew that I should — but when we came into Uncle David's room it was all I could do to stay there with John.

My uncle lay on a narrow chrome bed with a white cover pulled up to his sagging chin. He gazed at us blankly as John greeted him with loud enthusiasm. "Dad! It's great to see you." John glanced at me. "Vicky?"

I knew my role. I was to smile, kiss Uncle David's cheek or squeeze his hand, then say something bracing and cheerful. Today I found it impossible to fulfill those requirements. I looked at the shrunken, pathetic frame of the surrogate father who had dominated my childhood with harsh discipline and even harsher criticism. His narrow cruelty had delineated my life. He had been the prototype of the religious bigots who attacked me now over the content of *The Erotic Muse.*

"Vicky?" said John.

"What does it matter what I do? Uncle David doesn't recognize me."

"We have to . . ." John made a helpless gesture.

"What? Go through the motions? Let everyone see we care?"

Even the anger in my voice didn't rouse Uncle David, who continued to stare vacantly out at the world from his ruined body.

John looked miserable. "It's *Dad,*" he said in explanation.

My quick anger faded into depression. "He's your father, not mine."

"He was like a father to you."

I felt defeated by my cousin's incomprehension. "Yes," I said. "I suppose he was."

But I did not move to touch him.

Christie was wearing a pair of lurid pink shorts and an equally startling green top. She ran a hand through her short blonde hair. "You don't *ever* lecture in academic dress? What about some sort of black robe?"

I had to laugh at her lugubrious expression. "Sorry."

"Reyne won't be happy. She wants a photograph of you lecturing a class, and if you won't wear anything special, you'll look just like everyone else."

She flashed me an appealing smile. "How about a mortarboard tilted over one eye?"

"How about forgetting the whole idea?"

"No can do. Reyne Kendall has spoken."

My students were already filing into the lecture hall to hear my pronouncements on *Wordsworth: a poet who lived too long.* Some made straight for the front rows, but a hard core of students filled the upper tiers of the raked seating, as though anxious for the opportunity to surreptitiously exit, should my lecture prove too boring or too erudite for their tastes.

I grinned at Christie. "Tell Reyne I categorically refused to cooperate."

She gestured towards one of the lower entry doors. "Tell her yourself, Victoria, if you dare."

Reyne came striding in with quick, confident steps, wearing not her usual jeans and shirt, but a deep green suit and a frothy white blouse. "To impress the Vice Chancellor," she said, catching my appraisal. "And it's not about you," she added. "I'm contributing to an article on the funding crisis in Australian universities."

I was very pleased to see her. I told myself this was a response to the electric aura of energy that surrounded her, but I knew it was something more. What that *more* might be I wasn't willing to explore, other than to admit that it included the possibility of close friendship and, perhaps, the daunting thought of unambiguous understanding.

While I checked my notes, Reyne and Christie consulted. I remembered Hugh's gossiping reference to Christie as bisexual, and for the first time I considered whether she and Reyne had been — or might be — lovers. The thought was uncomfortable, as though I'd inadvertently invaded some intimacy that had nothing to do with me. I glanced at the white face of the clock that measured the slow progress of lecture room time for restless students. "I'm starting right now."

Reyne smiled at me mockingly. "Ma'am!"

She and Christie moved to one side, Reyne taking a notebook from her shoulder bag, Christie adjusting a camera tripod. I looked up at the packed rows, now mostly full of young people who chattered together like birds. I felt safe, secure. This was my territory, and lecturing was my profession. "Thank you . . ." I said, and silence ran along the seated lines.

This particular lecture on Wordsworth was well-practiced and I paced it with comment and poetry so that its pattern fitted the hour exactly. I was fond of Wordsworth and read examples of his poetry with that special pleasure that comes from balanced words, each in their best places. Although conscious of the slight stir that Christie's photography caused, I'd almost forgotten Reyne's presence until she came up to me at the end of the lecture. As the sounds of shuffling feet and the hubbub of conversation released from the constraints of an hour's silence filled the room, I said, "Have you time for coffee? It's too noisy here to talk, and there'll be another lecture in a few minutes."

Christie had another assignment, so it was only Reyne and I who faced each other over the ugly laminex table in the staff room. "I enjoyed your lecture," she said. "It may surprise you, but I like poetry."

Although it did, I said, "Why should that surprise me?"

She shrugged. "I don't suppose liking poetry fits with your view of me."

This was too close to the mark, so I said, "What sort of poetry do you prefer?"

"Really modern stuff, mainly. Not your area at all."

I raised my eyebrows. "Indeed?"

Reyne laughed. "I should learn not to do that. You hate being categorized in any way, don't you?"

She'd had her dark hair cut and styled. It curled like a glossy helmet, and I had to resist touching my own hair, which I'd pulled back into my usual tight chignon. I suddenly resolved to have it styled, although I'd worn it the same way for years.

Remembering the latest *Millennium* I'd bought that morning, I said, "I read your article about discrimination against women and gays in the military. I thought it very fine."

She looked at me doubtfully. "Is this a critique? Are you going to add a rider?" I didn't understand what she meant, and when I frowned in puzzlement, she went on, "I mean, Victoria, it's not your kind of writing, is it? I'm a journalist — I don't write literature."

Feeling a guilty twinge because I *had* been surprised at the quality of her work, I said stoutly, "If you mean, do I think your writing is inferior because it's for a general audience, then you're wrong."

"I notice," she said with a note of asperity, "that

you're choosing your words carefully. You can't really think that what I do compares with work produced in the exalted halls of academe."

"Are you trying to pick a fight?"

My indulgent tone made her smile. "You know — I think I am."

"Please don't. I admire your writing. I couldn't do it."

"Would you want to?" The challenge was back in her voice.

I put my hand lightly on hers. "Peace?"

Reyne didn't move her hand. "Okay," she said slowly. Abruptly embarrassed by our physical contact, I removed my fingers. "Did you have some questions to ask about the lecture or my work at the university?"

My return to formality didn't throw her at all. She flipped open her notebook. "Just a few. About both."

When I got home, my answering machine was blinking aggressively. Before I listened to the three messages I collected Tao from where he was reclining in my little courtyard and gave him a snack — he demanded a different gourmet cat food every night — and then made myself a strong gin and tonic. I didn't usually drink during the week, but I felt an unsettling combination of fatigue and restlessness that I hoped alcohol might assuage.

The first message was from Zoe, who managed to sound both peremptory and conciliatory: "Victoria, Arthur and I do want to see you as soon as possible, and *definitely* before you go to Melbourne. And I've found some more stuff in Mum's things you'll want to look at. Call me when you get home."

The second was from Gerald: "Hi, it's me. Wondered if you'd be free for dinner tomorrow night — say, Italian? I'll try and catch you later this evening." There was a pause, then he said, "Love you."

The third message clicked on. Immediately recognizing the voice, I frowned. "This is Reyne. I meant to ask when I saw you this morning, but I wonder if you'd like to go to dinner tomorrow night . . ." A small sound of amusement. "And it's not a disguised interview, Victoria. This is a genuine, no-strings-attached invitation. I'll be out this evening, so please leave a message on my machine if you're interested."

I finished my drink, picked up the receiver and punched in a number. "Gerald? It's Victoria. I'm sorry, but I've got something on tomorrow . . ."

When Zoe called early the next morning I felt thick and uncoordinated. I'd slept badly and fragments of my dreams still circled just out of reach. There was one disconnected, repetitive episode I'd had for years: bright, bright lights and a deep voice saying repeatedly, "Be a good girl, Vicky. Be a good girl." That's all I could ever remember, but after I dreamed it I always felt the same baffled anger and depression.

"You didn't ring back," Zoe was saying accusingly.

I took a large gulp of coffee, hoping it would

clear the haze that enveloped me. "Zoe, I was tired last night. I didn't want to talk to anyone." Uncharacteristically, I added a sarcastic sting, "Even to my nearest and dearest."

"I see," said Zoe, obviously taken aback by my tone. "Well, I'm sorry to interrupt you now. Perhaps you could call me back later." It was unusual for me to ever have her at a disadvantage, and it didn't last long. "Of course, Victoria, I *was* calling because I thought you'd be interested in a box of stuff I found in the back of Mum's wardrobe when I was cleaning it out. I mean, it's all about *you* ..."

I felt a breath of disquiet. "What's in the box?"

I expected Zoe to sound deliberately vague, and she did. "Odds and ends.. but you'll want to see them." In case I'd lost interest, she added, "And there are some reels of old film."

"When can I come over?" I was disconcerted by the urgency in my voice. Surely it was only a collection of worthless memorabilia — but I found myself reacting as though it were something dangerous that I didn't want here, in my own house. "When can I come over?" I said again.

I'd been incautious enough to show my interest, so naturally, Zoe played hard to get. "I won't be free today. It'll have to be tomorrow at the earliest."

We set a time, and before she rang off, Zoe brought up the real reason for her call: "And Victoria — Arthur and I *would* like to have a quick talk with you about investing in the company ..."

Amid a full day of lectures and tutorials, by

mid-afternoon I'd shaken off the dark mood that was a hangover from my restless night and my absurd apprehension about the box Zoe had discovered. I was looking forward to seeing Reyne that evening, so when she called and said, "I'm afraid there's a problem about tonight," I felt a stab of sharp disappointment.

"We can make it some other time."

She chuckled. "I haven't told you what the problem *is*, yet. Are you that keen to get out of dinner with me?"

I matched her light tone. "It depends where we're going."

"That's the problem. I've got two important international calls coming in, and I want to be home to take them. I wondered if you would mind if we had dinner at my place, rather than going out?"

I felt ridiculously relieved that I would still be seeing her. "Do you want me to bring something?"

"Not a thing. Just tell me what you don't eat."

I could almost smile at that. During my childhood, if I didn't eat everything on my plate, I had to stay at the table until I did. Zoe and John, trained since babyhood, seemed able to consume anything, but I, as my aunt often pointed out, had been spoiled. Food that I hated, like lambs' brains or tripe, had to be eaten, even if I gagged at the taste. "There are children starving," Aunt Felice would say with narrowed eyes. "Children who would be *glad* to have everything on your plate." Then there'd be dark silence, while the enormity of my failure to eat every morsel was considered.

I said to Reyne, "I don't eat brains or tripe . . . or quail."

"Oh, damn!" she said. "Just what I planned to cook!"

Gerald came into my office as I packed up for the day. Running late, I was keen to get home and shower before I was due at Reyne's. And I had to spend some quality time with Tao, or he would take revenge with an extended feline sulk. "I'm just leaving . . ."

Only half-jokingly, he said, "It's obvious that soon I'll have to make an appointment to see you."

"I'm sorry. Publicity for the book's taking a lot of my time —"

"That bloody book! I wish you'd never written it."

We were both astonished by his vehemence. He was flushed, apparently from a mixture of embarrassment and anger.

After a moment I said firmly, "The book's done. It's written. I'm not going to apologize for it."

"Of course you're not. Forgive me." His voice was still sharp.

I'd never seen him like this, so I wasn't sure how to react. He ran a hand over his face, as though attempting to wipe out the emotion.

"Victoria, from my point of view everything seems to have changed between us since you published that book. What I mean is . . . you're different, *we're* different." He sighed. "I'd just like us back as we were before."

I did my best to hide my impatience to be gone. "Can we talk about it tomorrow?"

"Of course." He was almost his urbane self. "I can see you're in a hurry."

Usually I would have lingered for a few minutes to soothe and reassure him, but tonight I was, for me, quite ruthless. "Yes, I am," I said, gathering my things together and leaving him wearing an expression of surprise.

Reyne's apartment was full of clean lines and bright colors. French windows opened onto a huge balcony crowded with earthenware pots of flowering plants. Inside, ferns and palms were featured in the decor.

"I'm a thwarted gardener," she said as she showed me around. "One day I want a house with lots of ground so I can grow vegetables and fruit trees as well as everything else."

The first telephone call she expected came while we relaxed with pre-dinner drinks. Politeness dictated that I not sit staring at Reyne while she talked, so I took my white wine and wandered out onto the balcony. The evening was beautiful, with a light breeze and a hugely yellow full moon in the darkening sky. I leaned against the railing and looked back into the brightly lit room.

She was wearing blue jeans and a shirt, as was I — but her top was a lovely rich tangerine, whereas mine was pristine white. I thought of the first time I'd seen Reyne, at the harbor side restaurant, and how much I'd disliked her. What had changed me? She was the same: her gestures emphatic, her manner often arrogant, her dark gaze coolly confronting. Was *I* different in some way? Gerald certainly thought so . . .

Reyne threw back her head and laughed. I smiled involuntarily. I could almost hear the hum of her vitality. Suddenly I wanted to share it — that taste for life that reverberated around her. In contrast, I seemed constrained, subdued, only half-alive.

She put down the receiver, picked up her glass, and strode out to join me. "Hey, look at that moon."

I couldn't remember another occasion when I'd been so conscious of someone else's physical self. The earthenware pots left little room, and we stood close together against the railing. I could hear her breathing, feel the warmth radiating from her skin, see the strong lines of her face in the moonlight.

We stood silently for what seemed a long time, then Reyne moved abruptly. "I'd better put the pasta on, or we'll starve before it's ready."

Curiously, I felt diminished by her absence, as though we had an unspoken partnership that had strengthened, but did not intrude. I followed her inside, finishing off my wine in one long swallow. She grinned at me from the kitchen. "I didn't realize you were such a practiced drinker, Professor Woodson."

I felt unaccountably cheerful. "I could surprise you, Ms Kendall."

She nodded slowly. "I bet you could."

It was myself I was surprising. I felt a heady combination of excitement and anticipation and told myself I had no reason for either emotion. But of course, it was Reyne. I knew that the evening was spiced with my knowledge of her sexuality. I knew how to behave with Gerald, with all the men I had known ... but I had no preparation for this. It was not that I expected her to make any move towards me. It was that *I* found myself fascinated by her. Not a physical attraction, of course, but certainly an emotional one.

Reyne cooked the pasta to perfection and combined it with a beautiful light sauce. I ate with more appetite than usual, exhilarated to be in the company of someone with whom I felt so free to laugh, to say what I thought. We lingered over the table, chatting as if we'd known each other for years.

The evening was passing too quickly, and with regret I noted the time. "I should go, soon."

Reyne warmed me with her quick, "Not yet, surely?" She strode off into the kitchen. "I'm putting fresh coffee on to wake you up before you go."

"I'm not sleepy."

She laughed. "Well, to wake *me* up, then. I'm still waiting for that second international call."

As we sat opposite each other in lounge chairs I was reminded of the hotel in Brisbane. Extraordinarily, as though she'd read my mind, Reyne said, "You never did answer my question."

"Which one? You ask so many."

She smiled. "The one about marriage."

I shrugged. "It's not for me. That's all."

"Why?"

Suddenly furious with her for spoiling the evening with the question, I said tightly, "I'm better alone. That's the way it is." She continued to look at me steadily. I said, "Have you considered that no one ever asked me?"

"No, I didn't consider that."

I could feel my anger rising like a tide, and for once I didn't try to contain it. "I can't imagine myself married. I never could. And Reyne, I'm not a lesbian, if that's what you're thinking."

I stood, putting down my coffee carefully. "I must go."

Reyne had risen too, and was silently regarding me. I was horrified to find myself near to tears. I wanted to get away, to be alone.

"I'm sorry," she said softly. She stepped forward and put her arms around me. "I didn't mean to upset you."

I stood still within her light embrace, surrendering, for a moment, to the confusion of my contradictory emotions. I wanted to step back from her, and yet stay. I wanted to put my arms around her at the same time I knew I should push her away.

Reyne looked at my mouth, the weight of her glance searing. I inclined toward her, wanting and not wanting the kiss. What was a kiss? Not something irrevocable that would change me . . .

Her lips, warm, slightly open, brushed mine. I heard the breath hiss in my throat as her embrace tightened. "Yes," she said against my mouth. Her tongue was delicately probing. I tried to draw back, but her hand at the back of my head held me captive.

My consciousness kept spinning away, enticed by sensation. My heart beat heavily, weakening me. Reyne's mouth demanded obedience. Trying to shut my lips against her insistent tongue was futile — and I realized I didn't want her to stop.

She took her mouth from mine, but continued to

hold me tightly. Her ragged breathing intrigued, excited my imagination. I knew she was going to kiss me again and that I'd have no control, no authority. "Reyne, please don't . . ."

She released me immediately and stepped back. "Victoria?"

Unable to meet her eyes, I fumbled for my car keys. "I have to go."

I drove home carefully, my actions reflecting the deliberation of my thoughts. I analyzed the evening as if I were an uninvolved observer. When upset or frightened, I had always used this technique to calm myself. As I reached my driveway I remembered, absurdly, that I'd neglected to thank Reyne for dinner.

CHAPTER SEVEN

Zoe dumped the large cardboard box on her kitchen bench. It was dusty and tattered and the printing along the side indicated that it had once held men's riding boots. Oddly reluctant to remove the grimy cardboard lid, I said, "What's in it? Have you had a good look?"

"Just to check it was all stuff for you." Zoe's voice was offhand, but there was an undertone that made me look up.

"Is there something . . ."

"What? Something what?" Zoe's tone was

challenging. It was as though I was reading a script where my part made no sense because I didn't know some vital fact.

I said, "Is there something you're not telling me?"

"Of course not." Zoe's reply was as rapid as it was insincere. "Obviously Mum kept some of your parents' papers and photos. She put them away in the back of the wardrobe and forgot about them." She smiled brightly. "Do you want coffee? Tea?"

The box was a time bomb ticking on the bench. I gathered it up under one arm. "Thanks, but I've got to be back at the university by four." This wasn't true, but I had no scruples about a falsehood, as I sensed Zoe was as keen for me to go as I was to leave.

Driving back to the university I kept glancing at the inoffensive cardboard container on the seat beside me. Although I had no more classes, I didn't want to take it back to my house, feeling, in some obscure way, that it would contaminate the peace I'd created there.

Gerald was just unlocking his car as I drew up in the staff car park. He slammed the door and walked over to me. "Can we have that talk now?"

"I *am* busy . . ."

"Not too busy to talk about us. You're not going to fob me off."

His determined tone made me feel both angry and guilty. "Gerald, I *do* want to discuss everything, but . . ."

He took the cardboard box from me. "Let me carry that. I'll walk up with you."

Before I could protest, he'd turned and was striding towards the entrance of the building. I followed, half impatient, half relieved that he'd delayed my investigation of the box's contents.

In my office, he placed the box precisely in the center of my desk. "What is this?"

I was offhand. "Just some papers my aunt kept for me."

Gerald wasn't really interested. "Can I see you tonight? I'm not pushing, Victoria, but I'm really unhappy about the way things are between us."

For him to say this much was an indication of his strength of feeling. He was usually reticent about his emotions — a characteristic that had initially attracted me to him.

I glanced at the box. "I've got a lot of work to do . . ."

"Please. It's important to me."

I felt my will power leaking out of me like air from a punctured balloon. "All right, Gerald. Where and when?"

He was buoyed by my acquiescence. "Leave it to me. I'll pick you up about seven."

I waited until he'd walked down the corridor, then locked the door behind him.

The cardboard lid felt gritty and unpleasant and the jumble of papers and photographs equally disagreeable. I sorted through the contents, glancing briefly at each item. There were old receipts, business letters, a few personal letters and cards, mostly between my parents, my baptism certificate indicating I'd been christened *Victoria May*, yellowed newspaper clippings — some, joltingly, reports of the accident that had killed my parents — and a collection of family photographs, some loose and some in envelopes or folders. At the bottom of the box were two battered containers of Super-8 movie film.

I took out one reel and unrolled a section, holding it up to the light. Even squinting at the tiny images closely it was impossible to make any sense out of who or what was there. Each container had *Woodson Enterprises* stenciled across the brand-name of the film and a handwritten note in faded ink. One notation read, *K5 plus,* and the other, *K & FW.*

I put the film reels to one side, making a mental note to ask about locating an eight-millimeter projector. Although long superseded by videotape technology, some projectors existed, I presumed; some enthusiast would still have the means to play old movie reels. There was a chance the university library might have access to out-of-date projectors for film held in the archives.

Putting the two film reels into the bottom drawer of my desk, I began to sort the rest of the contents into three piles: photographs; personal cards and letters; other papers. Then I started with the personal communications, feeling like a voyeur as I skimmed through several frank love letters my parents had written to each other before they married. Faded cards celebrating birthdays, one commemorated their first wedding anniversary, others were *I'm sorry* or *I love you* cards for some incidents in their relationship. I found a small bundle of cards tied with ribbon that were about me: congratulations on my birth, some for different birthdays — including one with an inscription that made my throat close: *Daddy loves his little Vicky.*

Suddenly I couldn't bear to continue sorting through the items. I shoveled everything into three large manila envelopes and put them into the drawer with the film reels. Tomorrow would be soon enough to go through these mementos of the past.

Before I discarded the grubby cardboard box, I examined it closely. Had the riding boots it once contained belonged to my father? Or, more improbably, to my Uncle David? Apart from a brand name and size, the box had nothing to tell me and, obscurely, I didn't want it in my office, so I went to the trouble of taking it down the corridor to the large waste paper container in the photocopying room.

Back in my office, I started as my telephone gave a metallic burr. "Victoria? It's Reyne." She sounded uncharacteristically meek, almost tentative. "About last night . . ." She gave a small, impatient sigh. "You know, I rehearsed what I was going to say, and now I've lost it."

During a restless night, I'd rehearsed what to say too. I chose a cool but friendly tone. "Reyne, let's just forget anything happened. It was just one of those things."

"If that's the way you want to play it."

In contrast to the doubt in her voice, I was decisive. "It is."

There was a pause, then she was all business. "I know you're flying to Melbourne Friday for another literary luncheon and book shop appearance. I hadn't planned to be there, but now *Millennium* is sending me to cover the Eiesley trial verdict. I'm leaving this afternoon, but I'm sure I'll still be in Melbourne for the weekend, and as I do need to tidy up a few details about your early life, I'd like to see you, if possible."

It was my turn to pause. I wanted to resume our growing friendship. In a restless night of analyzing that embrace, that kiss, I'd decided that I'd inadvertently precipitated the situation. I didn't cast Reyne as a predatory lesbian bent on seducing me and felt sure she'd take her cue from my behavior. "That shouldn't be a problem. I'm staying at the Southern Cross. You can get in touch with me there."

She thanked me formally, then hung up. For a moment I felt obscurely resentful, as though she should have been friendlier, until I realized it would be embarrassing for us both if she were. Somehow we had to reestablish our relationship so that there'd be no future misunderstandings.

Misunderstandings? an inner voice said. *The kiss was given — and received.*

My phone rang. "Hugh Oliver here, Victoria. Just checking you're A-OK for Melbourne."

"I am."

My brevity didn't dampen Hugh's enthusiasm. "Great! And I want you to know I'll be with you every step of the way."

"That's a comfort, Hugh."

He chuckled at my dry tone. "Knew you'd be pleased. I've got your itinerary for the States, too. Need to go over it with you, but that can wait until we hit Melbourne." he cleared his throat. "Victoria, there is one little thing . . ."

I was immediately suspicious. "What?"

"It's excellent publicity, doesn't cost a cent and puts your name in the public eye . . ."

"Hugh . . ."

"It's in today's *Courier*. Pippa Blaine's got an item about you in her column." He hurried on before I could comment. "This is the *second* time she's mentioned you, Victoria, *and* she's used a photo. You just can't buy that kind of coverage."

"What exactly does she say?"

"I'll fax it through to you, if you like." I had the feeling he didn't want to say it aloud because he knew I'd be unhappy with the text. "It's not necessary to fax it. Just read it to me, please."

Hugh cleared his throat again. "Well, all right . . ."

" 'The Professor of Sex Wooed,' the headline says. 'Word around university corridors is that attractive dark-haired Professor Victoria Woodson, writer of steamy bestseller, *The Erotic Muse*, will be hearing wedding bells any moment. Friends and colleagues confirm things are hotting up between the never-married prof and handsome historian Gerald Humphries. Who said all that dry research into sex never pays off?' "

I listened as he read it, sighed, and said, "Where did she get *that* from?"

Hugh was heartened by my mild tone. "Who knows where Pippa gets her material? She asks around, someone gossips, a few phone calls . . ." When I didn't respond, he added anxiously, "It is good publicity, Victoria. Trust me on this."

"Don't fax it to me, Hugh. I don't want anyone in the office reading it first and then sniggering when they hand it to me."

"I think you're taking this a little too seriously. And it's true, anyway, isn't it?"

I ignored his question. "I'll get my own copy. Don't bother sending me one."

I'd hardly got him off the line before Jane, a friend from Administration who'd been at the university so long she was almost a fixture, put her head around the door. "Seen the *Courier*, Victoria? Think you should."

"I didn't know you read that rag."

Jane's face crinkled with amusement as she handed me a copy of the tabloid newspaper. "Naturally I don't. It was the office staff."

I groaned. "God. Now I suppose everyone'll hear about it."

"Including Gerald Humphries," said Jane cheerfully, pointing to the center of the *Lifestyle* column. "When I left there was friendly competition in the office to see who should be the bearer of such good tidings."

I quickly read the paragraph to check that Hugh hadn't edited the version he'd read to me.

Jane's expression was sympathetic. "I can imagine how you feel, but you can hardly sue Pippa Blaine for telling the truth, however badly she writes it."

"It isn't true, Jane. To use the old cliche, Gerald and I are just good friends."

She grinned at me wickedly. "Of course you are. Just keep saying that. Maybe someone, somewhere, will believe you."

I was discovering that the most unlikely people believed tabloid newspaper gossip. Before I left for the day, the Vice Chancellor popped into my office to say cheerily, "Just happened to hear about Pippa Blaine's column. Are congratulations in order?" He seemed quite taken aback at my curt denial. Then, as I drove through the university security gates, the guard winked at me suggestively as he gestured with a *Courier* open at the appropriate page. At home I found two messages on my answering machine. In the first Zoe demanded to know why I hadn't told her the good news before it appeared in print. The second one, from my cousin John, simply asked if the rumor had any basis.

"Do *you* have anything to say?" I inquired of Tao, who had hurtled through the cat door when he heard the key in the lock. He had — but it was all on the subject of how he'd been neglected, and how food would lessen the trauma.

Knowing Zoe would pepper my answering machine with queries until I responded, I called her back immediately. "I didn't know you read the *Courier*, Zoe."

"I don't, usually. It was just by chance that paragraph about you and Gerald caught my eye." She went on the offensive. "Honestly, Victoria, I would have expected you to tell the family the news before some tacky gossip column prints it."

"I hate to disappoint you, but it isn't true."

Zoe clicked her tongue impatiently. "It's perfectly clear to me that Gerald loves you. And you're not getting any younger ..."

John was far more supportive. "I'd be annoyed, too, Vicky, but you have the consolation that it'll all be forgotten by tomorrow."

Gerald arrived precisely at seven. He kissed my cheek, then straightened his tie. "I didn't call you, Victoria. I was sure you'd realize I'd hear about the article and I knew we could discuss it tonight."

He looked subtly pleased, a fact that annoyed me further. "It isn't an article, Gerald. It's a paragraph in a cheap gossip column."

"No one will take it seriously and you have to admit it can't hurt your book sales."

"You're beginning to sound like Hugh."

My comment gained a slight grimace. "I certainly don't have any ambition to resemble Hugh Oliver. And you won't have to put up with anyone like him once the whole fuss about your book dies down."

"You'd like that, wouldn't you?"

He looked at me seriously. "I won't pretend I haven't resented the time all this has taken away from us, but I've thought it through, and I know I've been unreasonable."

I had the keen sense that no matter what I said or did, Gerald would refuse to argue with me. He was determined, it seemed, to be agreeable, even when I grumbled ungraciously about going out to dinner. "Gerald, I've got so much to do. I'm spending the weekend in Melbourne, and I haven't even thought about what I'm going to pack . . ."

"I promise to have you back early."

Ashamed of my churlishness, I made a mental vow to make the evening a success.

We dined at a little Italian restaurant that had both atmosphere and delicious food. Chatting lightly about work matters and mutual friends made me aware that most of my friends and acquaintances were associated with my work at the university. No doubt this was why Reyne Kendall seemed so dangerously different and why she intrigued me so much.

Gerald was at his entertaining best and we laughed the evening away. As he promised, he had me at my front door before eleven. I put the key in the lock, then turned to give him a good night embrace that would make it clear I wasn't asking him in, but he said quickly, "You did promise to talk seriously. I'm asking for a cup of coffee and half an hour."

Tao chose this moment to wind himself between my legs with purring expressions of deep affection. "He loves you," said Gerald with the clear intention of suggesting that Tao wasn't the only one to feel this emotion. Exasperated, I swept Tao up into my arms. "All right, thirty minutes and coffee. It's a deal."

While I filled the percolator, Gerald tried unsuccessfully to interest Tao in a game. I wondered if Reyne liked cats. I was convinced that anyone who had the slightest inclination towards them would fall instantly in love with Tao's sleek lines and aristocratic air. Even as a kitten he'd had an elegant high regard for himself, and his self-image had only intensified with adulthood.

Gerald waited until we both had mugs of coffee and were seated, carefully apart. Looking solemn, he ran a hand over his thinning hair. "Victoria, I think we should be married."

I felt frustrated by his good nature and his

imperviousness to my moods, to what I said and felt. I said in a reasonable, conversational tone, "Why do you want to marry me? I haven't got enough to offer you. I can't share things the way others do."

"It's *you* I want."

"That isn't a very convincing reason to change what we have."

He was prepared to argue his case. "Marriage is a *commitment*. It's not just being with someone. We'll solve our problems together. I'm not saying there won't be difficulties, but we start with the basis of a sound relationship because we have the same interests, the same views . . ." When I didn't speak, he said, passionately, "I *love* you."

I knew he wanted me to say that I loved him too, but it was an impossible statement. I didn't, couldn't, love anybody — at least, not in the way he meant. Miserable, awkward, I said, "To love someone means you want to go to bed with them, have sex with them. You must realize by now that's . . . not important to me."

He leaned forward to put his hand over mine. "Darling, it's not so big a problem that it can't be fixed. We'll work on it together."

"It's not like learning to ski, or developing a good backhand in tennis!"

He smiled faintly at my intensity. "I love you," he said quietly. "I love you enough for both of us."

"Don't — please."

Gerald didn't ask for clarification. He nodded soberly. "You're tired. We both are. Don't come to any sudden decision. Just know I love you and I'll wait for you."

I felt trapped, held fast by tentacles of his longing. "I don't want you to wait for me."

He shrugged. "Victoria, it doesn't matter what you say — I can't help it."

CHAPTER EIGHT

The first newspaper clipping had been precisely cut out and neatly folded. Now its yellowing paper was splitting along the lines of the folds. The photograph of the crash site was blurred and confusing, but the newsprint was still clear:

TWO DIE IN CRASH FIRE
Tragedy Orphans Little Daughter
A fiery death awaited Isabelle Woodson (32) and husband Frank Woodson (41) yesterday when their car left a straight stretch of country road near

Wiseman's Ferry, plunged over an embankment and struck a tree. The bodies, burnt almost beyond recognition, had to be cut from the wreckage. Their only child, young daughter (Victoria, 7) was spending the day with relatives and so escaped the inferno.

The second clipping was obviously from a suburban newspaper:

BUSINESSMAN INCINERATED

Well-known local businessman, Frank Woodson, was killed in a tragic accident last Sunday when his car ran off the road and burst into flames near Wiseman's Ferry. There were no witnesses to the tragic crash, which also claimed the life of his wife, Isabelle. Woodson was President of the Chamber of Commerce for the last two years, and his company, Woodson Enterprises, which distributes a wide range of training films for business, sport and pleasure, is one of the success stories of our area. Frank is survived by seven-year-old daughter, Victoria, who is being cared for by relatives.

The last clipping mentioned my parents only in passing. Headlined FATIGUE A KILLER, it went on to warn about "the too often disregarded factor in fatal car accidents of driver fatigue," and in the sad catalog of fatalities and other crash statistics, my mother and father's accident was listed.

It must have been my Aunt Felice who clipped out each item and put it away. I wondered why she had kept them, because when I was growing up, any time I'd asked her about my parents her face had grown stony and she'd avoided detailed answers. I could understand her not telling a child the full story about the crash and fire, but even when I was an adult Aunt Felice had remained reticent. I glanced at the clippings again. If they had been kept for me, along with the other papers, why hadn't I been given them long ago? Perhaps she'd decided they were too upsetting . . . or maybe she'd forgotten that they even existed.

I sat back with a sigh. The in-tray on my desk was stacked with papers. The top memo announced URGENT in red letters, but I didn't take the time to read it, especially since its source was Administration. Anything genuinely urgent would have been imparted by the efficient verbal network that covered the entire university. This unofficial system had ensured that everyone I met that morning believed that I faced imminent marriage to Gerald.

Swiveling my chair to stare out at the windy day, I tried to remember the recurring dreams that had filled my sleep with disquiet, and sometimes terror. Images solidified, then dissolved. I was a young woman dressed in a dazzling white dress with a scarlet sash across the breast, cowering as Uncle David hissed between thin lips: "You're evil! Evil! You were born to sin." I was an adult, consumed with unfamiliar desire, holding out my arms to a faceless, nameless person. I was a little girl, drenched with shame, crying while the bright light poured down on my nakedness. I was kissing Reyne, held safe in her arms . . . until she pushed me away.

I turned back to my desk, checked a number, and punched it in. I wasn't sure I'd get my cousin, who was an insurance assessor and therefore constantly in and out of his car, but John answered on the first ring. The background noise of traffic through his car phone didn't hide his enthusiasm. "Vicky! This is an unaccustomed pleasure — speaking to you twice in twenty-four hours."

Now that I had him on the line, I wasn't sure what to say. "John, I've got a favor to ask . . ."

"You've got it, whatever it is."

I smiled at his trust. "It might be something you don't want to do."

"What is it?"

"Zoe's given me a box of papers and photos concerning my parents. Since you're older than me, you're more likely to remember things, and I've got a few questions . . ."

"Do you want to sit down and talk it over?"

"Yes, but I'm out of Sydney for the weekend, and tonight I have to pack and try to finish off university work . . ."

His voice on the car phone faded then strengthened. "Are you lecturing this morning? No? I'm on my way to a job not far from the uni, so I'll call when I'm finished and see if you're free."

"Thank you," I told him warmly.

An hour later we met in the university cafeteria, ordered sandwiches and coffee, then went outside to sit in the sweet summer air. John was grave and, I thought, reluctant to give his memories too much weight. "When you came to us, Zoe was eight and I was thirteen-and-a-half."

"So you'd remember things I couldn't."

John half-smiled at my quick words. "At thirteen I was old enough to remember people and events, but not to really understand what was going on. I don't think I can be much help, Vicky."

"But my father was your uncle, your father's brother. You must have seen him and my mother fairly often."

John reflected as he chewed on a sandwich. "I don't think I can add anything to what I've ever said before. I remember Auntie Isabelle as quiet, but strong, if you know what I mean. I liked her because she treated me like a grown up, and would always take the time to sit down and talk."

"Did you like my father?"

My cousin frowned over the question. "I suppose I did. My picture of him is of someone loud, enthusiastic. He was the younger brother and Dad always used to say he was spoiled as a child."

"What did *you* think of him?"

"He always wanted to be out doing something — flying a kite or playing touch football." He narrowed his eyes in thought. "I don't think Mum really approved of him, somehow."

I handed him photocopies I'd made of the newspaper clippings. He read the articles with his usual methodical care, then handed them back. "Vicky, it isn't any good worrying about the past. Just forget it."

"I feel as though you're avoiding something. What aren't you telling me?"

His face was creased with concern. "I don't know anything I haven't told you."

"What about the accident? Aunt Felice would never discuss it with me, but she kept newspaper clippings. I don't even know how it happened . . ."

"No one knows how it happened. The car just ran off the road."

"There must have been an inquest — at the very least, a police report."

He shrugged. "I'm sure there was, but all I can tell you is that the accident wasn't discussed at home." He touched my hand. "If no other reason, we didn't mention it because *you* were there."

Still puzzling over the crash, I said, "Was my father a good driver? Were you ever in a car with him?"

"Doesn't matter, does it?"

"What?"

"I thought you knew. It was your mother who was driving."

Zoe snatched up the phone with an impatient, "Yes?"

"It's Victoria. I've just been talking to John about my parents' car crash."

There was a fractional pause before she said briskly, "I'm just on my way out. I'll call you later."

"Just one thing. When did you find out my mother was driving the car when it crashed?"

She gave an irritable sigh. "Mum told me — not long before she died, actually."

"Why didn't you tell me?"

"Why *would* I? What was the point? You didn't need to be told things from the past that might upset you."

With certainty, I said, "There's more, isn't there?"

"I don't know what you mean," she snapped. "I haven't got time to talk, Victoria. If you want to continue this later — fine — but right now I'm running late . . ."

I knew Zoe well enough not to persist, but I managed to extract a promise from her to meet early in the next week when I was back from the promotional trip to Melbourne.

For so long the past had seemed unimportant, inconsequential. Now it seemed full of unexploded mines. Questions boiled in my mind, and no one but John and Zoe could supply the answers. I'd never met any of my parents' friends and I had no relatives who'd known my mother and father. There was Uncle David, but although he had some lucid moments, I doubted if I could rely on the fragments of his memory for information.

Christie grinned at me. "It's certainly not *my* bright idea to drag you into the city to photograph you in a room full of matching leatherbound books, but the editor insisted."

I glared at the shelves of heavy tomes arrayed behind me. "These are *law* books, Christie, not literature."

She fiddled with her camera. "So who'll know? The idea's to contrast your modern image with the literature of ages looking down on you. Any old, impressive books will do."

The university library had many leatherbound reference books, but no one section held anything like the row after row of subdued leather jackets with discreet gold lettering that sat on richly polished shelves.

I checked my watch. "I don't want to miss my plane."

My complaint earned a placatory gesture. "Relax. I'm driving you to the airport as soon as I finish here."

"Friday afternoon traffic can be heavy . . ."

Christie was regarding me critically. "You're going to blend in with the books too much."

"You saying I look like an ancient tome?"

"Not so ancient, Victoria, and I do like your new hair style, but I did ask you to wear something bright."

I looked at Christie's fluorescent pink shirt. "I don't have anything quite that arresting," I said tartly.

"No matter." She rummaged in her bag. "I brought along a few things to add a bit of color."

I was wearing a dark blue dress cut on simple lines. In a few moments Christie had arranged a brilliantly patterned scarf at the neckline. "Don't argue," she said, "I know what I'm doing."

While she was checking camera angles I said, "I'm getting to see a lot of Reyne. She's already in Melbourne covering the Eiesley trial."

"Hope Vera Eiesley gets off."

It was a sensational murder trial, with a mother accused of killing her local priest when she discovered his long-term sexual abuse of her son. The case had generated intense media attention. A well-organized support group for Vera Eiesley had embarked on a fruitless campaign to have her murder charge reduced to manslaughter. The final summing up of the trial was today, Friday, and the jury was expected to begin deliberations during the afternoon.

I tried to imagine what it would be like to be in jail for years, enduring all the petty indignities and loss of privacy. "Juries don't often accept temporary insanity as a valid defense."

Christie snorted. "Frankly, in her place I would have killed him myself, and expected to be congratulated for it." She grinned at me. "But then, I never pretended to be well-balanced like Reyne. She can always see both sides of a question."

"She can?" I said doubtfully. Reyne had seemed to me to be a person of deep, hard-held convictions.

"I don't mean she doesn't have strong opinions of her own. She never lets them get in the way when she's doing a story. Reyne can achieve something I've never claimed to have — objectivity."

I raised my eyebrows. "About everything?"

There was a knowing edge to Christie's smile. "Except when she's in love."

Disconcerted by the turn the conversation had taken, I made a vague affirmative sound. Christie began to take photographs, talking as she did so. "Actually Reyne's only been back to her usual self for the last few months — turn your head a little to the left, please — since she broke up with Geraldine . . ."

I found I was keenly interested in what she was saying. "Mmmmm?" I murmured as an encouragement.

My prompting wasn't necessary. Christie said freely, "The actor, Geraldine Cornwell. Reyne took it hard when they broke up eighteen months ago."

I recognized the name, having seen Geraldine Cornwell in several stage productions. She was not only beautiful, but her acting had an intense, vulnerable edge that caught at the heart. "Were she and Reyne together long?"

Christie didn't answer until she'd arranged me to her satisfaction. Squeezing off another series of shots, she said, "Four, five years."

Although I wanted to know more, I didn't want to appear too eager. I said offhandedly, "Longer than many marriages."

"It *was* a marriage, Victoria. Not in the strictly legal sense, perhaps, but a marriage nevertheless."

Although the hint of censure in her voice decided me that a change of topic would be wise, I heard myself saying, "Why did they break up?"

"Irreconcilable differences, as the saying goes." She put down the camera and surveyed me deliberately. "But you'll have to ask Reyne herself . . . if you really want to know all the details."

CHAPTER NINE

Hugh Oliver had the same need to fill silence with conversation as Leila had demonstrated. Something about publicity must attract people who were either alarmed by quietness, or were challenged to fill an empty space with an avalanche of words. I endured a non-stop dialogue from Hugh during the hour or so it took to fly to Melbourne, then he talked in the limousine Rampion Press had provided, continuing our one-sided conversation right up to the door of my hotel room.

"No, Hugh, I'm too tired to get changed and then

go out for dinner. I'm going to get room service and have an early night."

Hugh was not happy to have me escape. "But, Victoria, there are Rampion executives here you should meet." He gave me his most winning smile. "You'll feel much better after you have a chance to freshen up." He tried his little-boy look. "And I did happen to mention that you'd probably be available."

"You didn't mention it to me. And I'm not." To forestall further discussion, I added firmly, "I've got a copy of the schedule and I'll be ready on time in the morning. I'll see you then, Hugh."

It gave me great satisfaction to close the door on his concerned face, and to luxuriate in the silence. I thought with pleasure of an evening alone. I'd deliberately left work papers behind and had brought a new novel that for weeks I'd been promising myself to read. First I rewarded myself with a long, hot bath.

The telephone rang while I wallowed in the water's soothing caress. I grinned, thinking of Hugh at the other end of the line poised to make one last fruitless attempt at persuading me to leave the sanctuary of my room.

A red *Message Waiting* light was blinking discreetly on the handset when I emerged wrapped in the hotel's thick white bathrobe. Although tempted to ignore it — surely it was only Hugh — I finally picked up the handset. I was unprepared for the jolt of pleasure when I found it was a message from Reyne asking me to call her at her hotel.

I tried to analyze my reaction as I waited to be

connected to her room. It was probably, I thought wryly, caused by sheer relief that the message wasn't from Hugh.

"Victoria? Now don't tell me Rampion's got you working tonight. I'm unexpectedly free, and I thought we might have dinner, if you were available."

I smiled at the familiar cadence of her voice. "Hugh did his best to rope me into something, but he retired hurt when I said I was too tired and was going to indulge myself with room service."

"Would you like a partner?"

"Pardon?"

Reyne chuckled. "I meant I'd join you for room service, if you don't feel like going out." When I didn't reply immediately, her confident tone became tentative. "I'm sorry, I didn't think . . . You must be tired . . ."

My temperate evening had suddenly taken on a glow of warmth. "I think it's a great idea. How long will you be?"

The wait for Reyne to arrive had a curious quality — calm anticipation of subdued delight. I knew very well that I should be cautious. After that kiss at our last meeting, she might place a wrong interpretation on my friendliness, but I resolutely put this thought to one side. I dressed in casual clothes, brushed my hair into the clean lines of its new, shorter style, examined my face critically in the bathroom mirror. I didn't look quite the same. Somehow my expression was more relaxed, less guarded.

We didn't touch when Reyne arrived, although I

wanted to give her a light hug, to say that she made a difference to me — though if I'd been asked, I knew I couldn't explain what it might be.

Any diffidence she had shown on the phone was gone. Her assured self-confidence had returned. She measured me with a long look. "I like your hair. It suits you short."

Brushing the compliment aside before it could embarrass me, I said quickly, "It was time for a change."

"You're changing a lot of things, aren't you, Victoria?"

I liked the way she said my name, crisply. "Things change, but I'm still the same."

She smiled, but didn't reply. I felt obscurely disturbed, as though I should have given another answer, so I said hurriedly, "Here's the room service menu."

We ordered extravagantly, and then talked about the Eiesley trial while we waited. Reyne's brief was to examine the impact of the trial and verdict from the point of view of the Church, which had been rocked with sexual scandals both in Australia and overseas, similar to the one that had led to the murder. "You can see why members of the Church hierarchy have made such a fuss over the religious erotica you examine in your book," Reyne said. "They have a long-standing policy of denial where sexual matters are concerned, and when it's actually sexual abuse, they turn their faces the other way and hope it will all go away."

"How can anyone ignore the abuse of children?"

My voice rang loudly in the room. Abashed, I said, "I'm sorry. It's something I feel strongly about."

There was knock at the door. The waiter steered in the wheeled table with impressive speed, then set it up for dining with a flourish of silverware and a haughty expression. I almost expected to hear dramatic music as he presented the wine for my approval, then removed the cork with showy expertise.

"We ordered far too much," said Reyne after he left. She smiled at me across the table. "It's fun, isn't it?"

And it *was* fun. I felt the satisfaction of doing something self-indulgent with a companion to share the guilt — not that Reyne seemed even slightly penitent about the size of the feast we were consuming.

As it had at her apartment, the time was passing too quickly. When we'd both eaten our fill, Reyne surveyed the table with satisfaction. "Let's push this out into the corridor for collection. Otherwise it'll sit here as a silent reproach for our gluttony."

Giggling like school kids, we maneuvered the laden table through the door. Reyne dusted her hands. "Mission accomplished."

Abruptly, unexpectedly, I wanted her arms around me again. "Reyne ..."

She seemed to read something in my face. Without a word she embraced me, holding me tightly so that I could feel the steady beat of her heart.

"I don't know ..." I said, as though she'd asked me a question.

She kissed me with care, then simply held me. I

was in a dream, not of passion, but of nameless longing. "Don't stop," I breathed against her cheek, needing the heat of her mouth again.

"Are you sure?"

"Yes."

She laughed softly. "And if I want something from you, will you give it to me?"

"Yes." I could have added, "Anything you ask," so reckless was I for the taste of her mouth again.

Gentleness gone, she forced her tongue between my lips. When men had kissed me this way I'd recoiled at the need they displayed. When it was Reyne, I devoured her with equal ardor.

She was undoing my bra, sliding her fingers over my breasts. It distracted, annoyed me. "No."

Her hands stilled. When she stepped back from me her eyes were dark, her skin flushed. I was staring at her mouth, wanting her to kiss me again. Her lips curved in a smile that seemed half-resigned, half-bitter. "No, Victoria. A kiss isn't enough. Not for me."

Disappointed anger made my voice shake. "You're playing games, Reyne."

"*I'm* playing games?"

She was impatient to be gone, gathering her things swiftly and walking briskly to the door.

"Reyne . . . I'm sorry."

"So am I." She paused with her hand on the doorknob. "The pity of it is I've let myself get in so deep."

Chewing listlessly on a piece of toast, I glared at

the headlines of the fat Saturday morning paper. The jury was expected to reach a verdict today on Vera Eiesley's guilt or innocence. The journalist clearly believed that the verdict was so obvious that jury deliberations should not be longer than decency required.

I folded the paper and dumped it in the middle of the ruins of a room service breakfast. Squinting through the over-cheerful glare of the sun I could see the greenery of one of Melbourne's many beautiful parks.

The phone rang: it was Hugh bubbling with enthusiasm to start the day. I broke into his exuberant dialogue. "I'm almost ready. I'll meet you downstairs in fifteen minutes . . ."

Pacing morosely around the room wasn't going to assist my preparations for the day's interviews. I cleaned my teeth, tried to hide the dark circles under my eyes with makeup and contemplated the selection of clothes without interest. I wanted — needed — to talk with Reyne. To explain . . .

I snatched up the receiver, scarcely requiring to check the telephone number of Reyne's hotel — I'd started to dial it several times that morning, but stopped myself before the digits were complete. She didn't answer, and when the helpful hotel voice broke in after the seventh ring, I left a brief message asking her to call me.

The phone rang just as I replaced the receiver. "Victoria? I'm in the lobby and you're not. Where are you?" Hugh sounded both anxious and slightly outraged. "Are you going to be long? We'll be late if you don't hurry."

When I joined him ten minutes later he said

accusingly, "You've never been late before. In fact, you're always *early*."

"I'm sorry, Hugh. I slept in."

He accepted the lie with good grace. "You've been doing a lot, Victoria, what with your university work and all these appearances. We'll have to look after you. Make sure you don't wear yourself out . . ."

"Rampion Press *has* invested a lot in Victoria Woodson," I said acidly. "So it's essential I be kept in good condition."

Hugh looked worried. It was obvious he wanted to say something to placate, but couldn't quite decide what would be appropriate. He settled for a neutral sound and then a hurried comment on my first appearance on a morning television show. "Neville Tower just *loves* your work. I know you might think it unusual in a talk show host, but apparently he's really very interested in literature." Hugh flashed me a smile. "He's read *The Erotic Muse* cover to cover, not just the chapter headings and a few words here and there."

I was rapidly becoming an old hand at the activities associated with television programs. I sat patiently while television makeup was applied, and visualized the lines of Reyne's face. I waited obediently beside an earnest assistant director for my cue to enjoy my slice of electronic fame — and recreated the pressure of Reyne's lips. On the set, I watched Neville Tower's bouffant hairstyle while he smiled at the camera, and remembered the texture of Reyne's hair.

When I came off the set, Hugh was waiting for me. "Victoria, you're not . . ." He searched for a non-wounding phrase. "... you're not quite *with it* this morning. Do you know what I mean?"

"You'd better tell me, Hugh."

He patted my shoulder. "No harm done, but I did get the feeling you weren't really concentrating ... Neville *did* have to ask you a couple of questions more than once before you responded ..."

He broke off as the monitor above our heads showed an advertisement for a weight loss clinic fade out, but instead of returning to Neville and his next guest, it went to a newsflash.

"The verdict!" The woman on the screen looked well satisfied, as though she'd personally created the event. "The jury's back to deliver the verdict Vera Eiesley holds her breath to hear," she stated confidently. "We're crossing live to our Steve Wax ..."

Her hard glossiness was replaced by the soft good looks of a young man who had posed himself in front of the facade of the criminal courts building. "Well, Denise," he said portentously, "it looks as if the jury's gone against every prediction and believed the defence of temporary insanity. Vera Eiesley's been found not guilty of the willful murder of her parish priest ..."

I scanned the crowd behind the young man, hoping, although not believing, that I'd see Reyne there. It was a waste of time, but I persisted, half listening to the newscast. "And how will Vera be feeling at this point in time?" was the fatuous question from the smiling anchorwoman.

"What a stupid question," said Hugh, as though he'd never been guilty of articulating anything of similar banality. He glanced at his watch. "Come on, we've got a schedule to keep."

I was bored and tired by the time Hugh released me into the tranquility of my hotel room to prepare for a reception in the evening. There'd been no message from Reyne and I sank, dispirited, onto the bed. Tomorrow would be more of the same, starting with a reporter from what Hugh called *the mega-selling women's magazine of all time.* "It's a coup!" were his last words on the subject, after he warned me, "Don't be *too* controversial ... just a touch ..."

When the phone rang I was so sure it was Hugh I said abruptly, "Yes? What is it?"

"That rather depends on you," said Reyne.

"I'm sorry, I thought was Hugh." Ridiculously, I added quickly, "Don't hang up."

"I got your message to call." Her voice was neutral, as though whatever I had to say was of little interest.

I knew what I should say — some careful, balanced comment. Instead I blurted out, "I was miserable after last night. I need to see you again."

"All right, but I'm pretty tied up — and so are you from what I remember of your schedule. Will tomorrow do?"

"Whatever suits you."

My sharp disappointment must have been evident because Reyne said, "I'll try and make it to your reception tonight, but it won't be until quite late. If I miss you, I'll leave a message at your hotel." She gave a short, bitter laugh. "I've no idea why I'm doing this. Have you?"

"No," I said, for the moment simply content that I would be seeing her.

The function was largely for what Hugh rather dismissively called "literary types." Among the writers there were some I admired, along with a few I privately considered to be merely adroit self-promoters. The rest of the gathering was made up of people associated with publishing — press journalists and a small sprinkling of critics.

One influential critic, renowned for panning anything written by those outside a particular literary group — I had received a vitriolic review — swanned over to me with an ingratiating smile. "Professor Woodson! I do hope you've got something in the literary works just a tiny bit more *weighty* than the *Muse.* I mean, it was *fun,* but not really *serious* writing.'

"I consider it among my best work," I said levelly.

"Indeed?"

Hugh materialized beside me. "Sorry to interrupt, but you're needed, Victoria." As he steered me towards a knot of people in animated conversation, he said, "Thought a rescue was in order."

"I didn't need rescuing."

"Not *you,*" he laughed. "I was rescuing the doyen of literary criticism from annihilation."

"That's quite an exaggeration. We were just chatting."

Hugh snorted his amusement. "Even from across

the room I could see the formidable Professor Woodson gearing up for battle. I thought it would be wise to intervene before you drew blood."

It often puzzled me why I was so often described as tough or intimidating. "I'd only said a couple of words. What was so formidable about that?"

Hugh shrugged. "I don't know . . . something about the way you act. As though you feel secure enough not to care what people think of you."

I smiled wryly at his comment. Most of the time it was true — I didn't allow myself to get close enough to anyone for it to matter too much about the person's opinion. But I cared what Reyne thought of me — so deeply it was like a pain.

The evening to me was a blur of talking faces, snatches of conversation, politely insincere comments, a few moments of genuine pleasure when meeting individuals I admired and respected — all of this punctuated by offerings of food that tasted identical, and mouthfuls of anonymously excellent wine. "We can leave any time you like," said Hugh, as I took a furtive glance at my watch.

"I'll stay a little longer," I said graciously.

I saw Reyne before she saw me. Wearing a simple black jacket and pants, she stood at one side systematically scanning the crowd. I was absurdly pleased that it was *me* she was looking for, and I had to restrain myself from smiling idiotically when she located me and waved an acknowledgement. With impatience I watched her make a slow path across the room. Every few steps someone called a greeting and she stopped to say a few words. Then, when she reached me, I wasn't sure what to say.

Reyne looked serious and rather tired. "You ready to go?" she said.

I nodded. "More than ready. I'll just tell Hugh I'll make my own way back to the hotel."

In the cab she gave the name of my hotel without consultation, then sat back and shut her eyes. It was a silence we didn't break until we reached my room. "I'll order coffee," I said, "or do you want something stronger?"

"Coffee. Anything else will send me to sleep."

Room service was commendably quick, which was fortunate because pouring the coffee gave me something to do, other than watch Reyne as she stood at the window looking down at the lights of the Saturday evening traffic.

"Are you going to come over here for your coffee, or shall I bring it to you at the window?"

She smiled faintly at the bite in my tone. "When you put it that way — I'll come over there." She took the cup I handed her, settled herself into the chair opposite me and said coolly, "You're calling the shots, Victoria."

"Last night . . ." I stopped, uncertain of what I wanted to say. She didn't rescue me, so I tried again. "I think I gave you the wrong impression last night."

Reyne gave an infinitesimal shrug. "Perhaps it was my fault. I didn't take Pippa Blaine's gossip column seriously."

"About Gerald Humphries? You were right not to believe it. We're the proverbial good friends."

Her sigh seemed to blend resignation and tiredness. She didn't look at me as she said, "I simply read the signs wrongly. I thought you were . . . interested."

"I *am,* but perhaps not the way you mean. I feel a great deal for you, I can't remember being this way about anyone before . . ."

Now she was looking at me, frowning slightly. "You kissed me. I thought you wanted more." She took a gulp of coffee. "You have to admit you gave me every indication you did."

It seemed to me that every word we exchanged added to the confusion I felt. "I don't understand!" I said passionately. "I don't know what I want, or don't want."

Reyne put down her cup. Her dark eyes seemed even darker. "Tell me when you find out."

I was terrified that she might go, that I'd never be able to recreate this moment when we might be able to share a true communication unclouded by civility and self-protection. "Reyne, please. I must explain. I've always been cold . . . frigid. Physical love doesn't mean anything to me. There's something wrong. Something missing in me."

There was bitterness in Reyne's voice. "And so you decided to experiment with a woman."

"If it were only that easy." I was immeasurably relieved to have actually put it into words. I looked at her and imagined her arms around me. "If I did — it'd be you."

"Don't say that!" She got up and began to pace around the room. "It isn't fair, Victoria," she said harshly. "I'm not about to become your sex therapist." She glared at me. "I was stupid enough to believe . . ." With an exasperated sigh she broke off.

"Believe what?"

"I was looking for a relationship. Someone important in my life. God knows why I thought it might be you." She turned to look for her things. "This is pointless. I'll go."

I couldn't believe the storm of emotion that had overtaken me. "Please, Reyne. Please don't go."

"Why not?"

"I feel . . . I don't understand what I feel . . ." I had to smile at the absurdity of it all. "Reyne, I don't know what it is — but it's for *you*. And it's so strong." When she didn't move or speak, I said, "I'd call it love, but that would be maudlin, wouldn't it?"

She smiled at me — the first genuine smile I'd had from her that evening. "It might be maudlin," she said, "but I quite like the sound of it."

CHAPTER TEN

I sailed through the early morning interview in my hotel room with the brittle, over-dressed reporter from the women's magazine. I wasn't even ruffled when she asked for "the woman's side of being a professor" and whether I had any tips for aspiring best selling authors, other than to "load the manuscript up with sex."

Reyne had only stayed a short while and had left after we'd agreed on a time for the interview on my early life that we'd discussed in Sydney. We hadn't embraced, but I felt much happier about our relationship. *Relationship:* it was a word of infinite possibilities — and threats.

Hugh was delighted by my change of mood — "See what a good night's sleep can do, Victoria" — and keen to review last-minute changes in schedule for my trip to the States.

"Hugh, we've already been through all this."

My protest made him purse his lips. "I don't want you to accuse me of not telling you everything."

"Have you sneaked in more appearances?"

"Well, since you're in New York for three days . . ."

"No."

Astonished, he repeated, "No?"

I had an ulterior motive for refusing more appearances in Rampion Press's home city. Reyne had told me last night that she was spending a week in New York visiting *Millenium's* head office, and as the time overlapped my visit, I wanted as much time free as possible so I would be able to see her.

"Hugh, Rampion's getting blood from me. I don't believe I need to do any more."

Looking sulky, he said, "You seem to forget they published your book."

I was suddenly impatient with him. "Hugh, Rampion Press has done very well out of *The Erotic Muse.* It wasn't printed out of charity. I'm willing to help promote it, but enough's enough."

"Okay," said Hugh, smiling brightly. I'd learned that he was as tenacious as a bulldog, so I expected him to return to the subject when I was jet-lagged, or maybe even slide the appearances into the schedule and not mention them.

"And don't," I said severely, "try to add anything without telling me."

"As if I would," he said, all injured innocence.

"You were seven when your parents died and you went to your aunt and uncle's?" Reyne's tone was businesslike and her expression one of professional interest.

I matched her attitude. Staring at the miniature recorder on the table between us, I said, "Yes. My parents died together in a car crash."

"Where were you when it happened?"

"With Aunt Felice and Uncle David — the relatives who brought me up — that day I'd been left there for some reason."

She flipped over a page in her notebook. I looked at her face intently, as though to print it on my mind. "Do you remember being told your parents were dead?"

"Only very vaguely. I doubt that Uncle David would think it his duty to tell me, and, knowing my Aunt Felice, she would have said something like, *Your mother and father have gone to heaven, Victoria,* and then carried on as usual."

Reyne looked up. "Not a warm, sympathetic woman?"

The description made me smile. "Not by the wildest stretch of the imagination."

"And your uncle?" She raised her eyebrows at my

succinct description of Uncle David. "He sounds a perfect husband for your aunt."

I felt embarrassed, as though I'd been disloyal. "Look, they did their best by me, and in case it sounds too grim, I did have my cousin John."

"I've met John. He's obviously very fond of you." She looked at me measuringly. "And I've interviewed your other cousin, Zoe."

"Yes, *Zoe.*" I made a face. "Zoe said she tried to protect my privacy, but basically I only had myself to blame if personal questions were being asked about me."

"She gave me some photographs." Reyne slid one across the polished surface. "Do you remember this being taken?"

I was immediately reminded of the photographs crammed into the envelope in my desk drawer. I hadn't looked at them again after the first hasty glance, because they disturbed me too much. Reluctantly, I picked up the black and white print. The images were crisp. I judged it'd been taken just before my parents died, because I looked very much as I did in the early photographs after I'd moved in with my aunt and uncle. "I've never seen this before," I said.

Frozen in what seemed to be a happy moment of time, I stood between my parents, smiling. My mother's arm was around my shoulders; my father stood slightly apart from us, hands behind his back. I could see traces of my mother's face in my adult features, but, apart from the dark springy hair, I could detect little resemblance between my father and myself.

I became unaccountably sad. "I don't remember anything about it." I turned it face down on the table. "Reyne, I'd rather you didn't use it in your article."

"Why? It's ideal. It's a really clear print, you look happy, both your parents are in it . . ."

"I don't want you to use it!"

She blinked at my vehemence. "Okay, but it's the best one of your parents I've seen."

"I don't want any of those early photographs in the article."

Reyne sat back. "Why not?"

I waved away the question. "I want to ask you something — this is nothing to do with the interview." When she nodded, I went on, "I want to get details about my parents' accident. It seems to me you'd know where I should start looking."

She was openly curious. "Any particular reason for your interest?"

It was a relief to tell someone outside the family. "For some reason, no one told me it was my *mother* driving when the car ran off the road. I didn't even know they'd been burnt to death until I was almost an adult. I can understand why a child wouldn't be given the details, but once I'd grown up . . ."

Reyne looked at me intently for a moment, then said, "Okay, give me any details you've got and I'll see what I can find out for you. There are newspaper morgues, of course, but I presume you want information from something official, like a police report or inquest."

"I'd be very grateful. John says I should forget the past, but . . ."

"It's always best to know. *Always.*"

128

I didn't argue with her confident words, but I was stingingly aware that there might be things in my past that might have the power to shatter my comfortable life.

I was irritated, rather than pleased, when Gerald met me at the airport. "Thought I'd surprise you."

"You have."

He wasn't the least put out by my ungrateful tone. "And you'll be delighted to know that Tao graciously accepted that I'd been deputized to feed and entertain him."

Immediately contrite, I took his arm. "You're such a good friend, Gerald."

The airport was full of people, all apparently in a hurry and most displaying either anxiety or resignation, both expressions appropriate for air travel. As we began to walk against the tide, he said, "Victoria, you know I want to be much more than a friend." Seeing my closed expression, he went on conversationally, "And who is looking after Tao while you romp around the United States? Do I win the prize again?"

"My next door neighbor has a niece who's willing to stay in my house and meet Tao's every whim."

Gerald found this amusing. "*No one* could meet Tao's every whim. He's the most demanding cat I've ever met."

"He is, isn't he?" I spoke more in admiration than censure, and Gerald smiled at me.

"You love that cat more than anything, don't you?"

"It's possible."

"I'd like to think one day you'd love me half as much."

He'd spoken lightly, but I felt the weight of his affection like a demand. "Let's get the luggage," I said.

In his car, I kept glancing at him. He was one of those people who always keep just under the speed limit and look with scornful superiority upon those unfortunate enough to be pulled over for traffic violations. I couldn't help comparing him to Reyne. Gerald was cautious and dependable — Reyne promised the exhilaration of life lived with the accelerator down to the floor.

Why couldn't my life continue as it had? Why wasn't I content with what, before, had been quite enough for mild happiness? Now I was restless, unfulfilled. I wanted more, much more. I craved companionship, love. But not the insipid, temperate affection that Gerald offered — it was the darker, deeper passion that Reyne represented that enticed me.

Passion? All I knew was an echo of passion, a shadow of physical delight. I believed Gerald would accept my limitations — he certainly had in the past — but Reyne? I could never believe she'd docilely agree to such inequality in our responses. She would always want me to share the sharp delights of passion . . . and I couldn't.

"What's wrong?" said Gerald. "You look positively miserable."

I could imagine his startled reaction if I told him my real thoughts . . . *I'm contemplating three life choices, Gerald: first, a socially acceptable marriage to dependable you; second, a lesbian relationship with exciting Reyne; third, the bland, and safe, alternative of leaving things just as they are now.*

"Just thinking of all the marking I should have done before I left for Melbourne," I said.

I had all of the old photographs spread out on my desk when the phone rang.

"I'm shopping in town this morning," said Zoe, "so I'll call into the university on my way. I should be there about ten. Are you going to be available?" Her tone made it obvious that she expected I would alter any previous engagements to accommodate her.

"Zoe, this is good of you —"

"Yes it is, Victoria. I don't approve of stirring up past unpleasantness, but if you insist . . ." Her tone made clear the unspoken conclusion to her sentence, *then you can suffer the consequences.*

She arrived on schedule, striding into my office with such indignant energy that her high heels left a line of indentations in the carpet. She didn't wait for a greeting. "What do you hope to gain from raking over the past?"

"Until a few days ago, I didn't know there *was* a past to rake over, Zoe."

Her irritation changed to a curious mixture of reluctance and sympathy. As she sat down — even this action an emphatic gesture on her part — she said, "I'll tell you anything I know, but I warn you, it isn't much." She mimicked deep thought, drumming her fingers on the armrest of the chair. I was sure, however, that Zoe knew exactly what she was going to say, so I didn't prompt her.

She took a deep breath. "Those last weeks before Mum died, she wanted to talk about the past, get a few things off her chest. We discussed lots of things that won't interest you, but she did keep returning to the day your parents died." She shot me a look. "You knew Mum — you had to drag things out of her if you wanted to know anything."

I sighed. "Please, Zoe, this is important to me. What did she tell you?"

Reyne called from the airport. "I'm back. Do you want to see me?"

My sudden joy showed in my voice. "Of course I do. When?"

"Tonight. I might have something on your parents' accident by then."

"I've seen Zoe, so I know something too."

I'd tried to sound offhand, but Reyne said, "Not good, obviously."

I wanted — needed — her comfort. "Come early, please."

For the rest of the day I plunged determinedly into work, burying my thoughts and feelings under an avalanche of marking, lecture preparation, faculty meetings and reading. I tossed aside a professional journal of impeccable tedium as Jane put her head around my door. "That Super-8 projector you wanted — I've organized it with Ted in the library. You want to use it there, or will I get him to bring it up to your office?"

I wanted to be alone when I viewed the two reels of film. "Can he deliver it here? I won't need it for long, and I'll use the wall for a screen."

Jane glanced at the wall. "Rubbish. I'll get you a screen. Now, do you want Ted to load the projector — he's hinted you'll never get it right — or will you wing it yourself?"

Somehow I was reluctant to let anyone else touch, let alone see, the film. "It can't be that difficult. I'm a professor, remember."

Jane grinned obediently at my levity. "Yeah," she said facetiously, "but don't forget you're a *woman*, too."

In quite another context, I thought about Jane's comment as I drove home. Reyne was a woman — a fact whose significance I'd hardly regarded up till now. During the course of my life I'd met homosexual people. I knew several lesbians, both as students and colleagues, and I couldn't remember ever giving their sexuality or their relationships more than a passing thought.

Of course, I had to admit with a wry smile, I'd hardly given *any* relationships more than a passing thought. But that wasn't the case now. Whatever I had with Reyne, it wasn't yet what others would call a relationship — but it already had the power to shake my ordered life and send my disciplined mind into areas never before explored.

I dissected relationships with an academic's skill. They were the stuff of literature — relationships successful and unsuccessful, calm or violent, equal or unequal, moderate or passionate. I'd written so confidently about love and passion as I'd studied the writings of others, yet when I was faced with actuality I realized I knew nothing that would guide me now.

Heart, mind and body. That would be what Reyne expected because that is what she would give me in return. It was a contract where *she* would always be short-changed.

I could only partly control my heart and mind. My body was unresponsive to my will where lovemaking was concerned. I'd wanted, in the past, to experience *something*, not necessarily the tumultuous physical reactions so beloved of popular literature, but even a flutter of response. Sometimes — rarely — when Gerald had been even more patient than usual, and I'd had enough alcohol, I'd felt the stirrings of desire. I recognized it intellectually, observing it in Gerald's labored breathing and cry of release. I doubted if I would ever feel — or need — that relief.

Tao had taken a liking to Reyne. When she arrived he deigned to be stroked and admired, and eventually packaged himself neatly on her lap and sank into a contemplative state, only twitching his whiskers irritably if she moved.

I watched Reyne sip her white wine as I nursed my gin and tonic. I didn't feel like drinking or eating. I just felt like sitting in quiet companionship. I'd meant to enjoy inconsequential conversation until the pizzas were delivered, but I surprised myself by saying baldly, "Christie told me about Geraldine Cornwell."

Reyne looked at me levelly. "Did she? Did you learn all you wanted to know?"

"I didn't want to know anything in particular." I knew I was blushing and that made me furious. "Christie volunteered the information. I didn't ask."

"Do you want to know what Gerry means to me now?"

"No," I said quickly, then, "Of course I do."

"I suppose I love her . . ."

I couldn't understand — or believe — what pain a few words could cause. I took a breath to make some commonplace comment to hide my injury, but before I could speak, Reyne went on, "But it's not like before. Now I feel a kind of regretful love, that we had so much . . . and it ended." She shrugged. "The cliche's true — you can't ever go back."

In the silence that followed I felt conflicting emotions: I was happy that Reyne didn't love as she had before; I was despairing that I could ever fill such a gap in anybody's life.

"To change the subject," said Reyne briskly, "I've got some information about your parents. There was an inquest, of course, because it was a case of violent death. The finding was inexplicable accident. The car was on a straight stretch of road, there were no skid marks and the weather was good."

"Zoe said her mother told her that my parents had a violent quarrel the day they died. My mother had actually walked out on my father a week or so before, had gone to stay with Uncle David and Aunt Felice."

Reyne nodded agreement. "That was raised at the inquest as a possible reason for your mother losing concentration and running off the road." She frowned. "I find it a bit strange that your mother would go to her husband's family for help, rather than to friends or relatives of her own."

"I'm sure she had friends, but no living relatives. Anyway, it was clear she was welcome there and my father wasn't. Zoe's mother said that when my father arrived and he and my mother had the heated argument, my Uncle David got involved and came close to physically attacking him. My mother prevented a fight by saying she'd go out with my father and discuss things."

"Do you know why your mother was driving?"

"My father'd been drinking. She insisted she should drive."

The story seemed remote, like some old black and white movie, until Reyne asked, "Do you have any idea what the argument was about?"

I felt inexplicably ashamed. "Yes. It was about *me*."

She looked puzzled. "Your parents were arguing about custody?"

I thought of how irritated Zoe had been when I'd hammered her with the same question. "Aunt Felice didn't give Zoe many details. She just said they were arguing violently about me."

Reyne frowned her dissatisfaction. "From memory, that isn't what your aunt said at the inquest. You weren't even mentioned."

"My aunt was a witness?" I asked in surprise.

"And your Uncle David. In their evidence they both implied that although there'd been considerable

136

conflict in your parents' marriage, the meeting that last Sunday was friendly, and they went off together to discuss a reconciliation."

Perplexed and frustrated, I stood and began to move aimlessly around the room. "Then why did my aunt tell Zoe that they were quarrelling violently about me?"

"Perhaps you'll never know, unless your uncle —"

"His mind's gone," I said harshly.

I felt cold, disconnected, full of sour unhappiness, and, as Reyne looked at me, I knew I couldn't bear her concern, her pity. I made my tone dismissive. "Reyne, I can't imagine why I'm making such a fuss about something that happened so long ago."

Tao complained bitterly as Reyne moved him from her lap. She came over to me and opened her arms.

Resentment spilled into my voice. "I'm not a baby to be comforted."

"Would you comfort *me,* if I needed comforting?"

I stepped, half unwilling, half yearning, into her embrace. "Do you ever need comforting, Reyne?"

"Often."

She seemed so strong to me, so sure of herself. "I can't believe that." The line of her mouth was enticing.

"Believe it," she said thickly. Her body was tense against me.

Her kiss was urgent, compelling, but I turned my head to break the contact. "This isn't going to work. I can't. You know I can't . . ."

She was sliding her palms over my back, her

fingers tracing patterns that made me shiver. I reached back and seized her hands. "Let me touch *you.*"

Reyne was breathing hard. "*I* don't need to be aroused. That should be clear to you."

"Please."

She was indulgently patient. "So what are we proving here? I can climax any time."

I put my hands under her jacket and pulled her against me. "God, you're so conceited," I said against her throat. She stood still, her reluctance plain. "Just to please me."

As she nodded agreement, I undid the fastening of her jeans, slid the zipper slowly down. She smiled lazily. "Going straight for the jackpot?"

"No. Not yet. Maybe not at all."

The power was exhilarating. My fingers traced fire on her skin, tightening her nipples under the thin material of her bra. "Undress me?" she said.

"You're so impatient."

We began to kiss again — deep, slow kisses. One part of me tried to observe with detached interest. Technically, I believed I knew what to do. I'd read enough erotica, both heterosexual and homosexual, to be an expert on the subject in an academic sense. But actuality was something very different. Nothing had prepared me for the smoothness of Reyne's skin, the heat of her body, the heavy beat of her pulse — nor for the response that was uncurling in me.

First, I thought it was the power that my mouth and hands had to arouse her that intoxicated me. But then I heard myself gasp, and realized that in the core of me a heat was growing — a demanding, exciting warmth that washed down my thighs, hollowed my stomach.

"Reyne!"

But as she pushed me gently back onto the bed the light from my reading lamp fell across my face like a slap. I pushed her away as she began to undress me. "No. Don't."

"I won't hurt you, Victoria. Just let me touch you."

I sat up. "I can't." I was crying, and I bent my head to hide my wet face. "Please forgive me, Reyne. I don't know why this is happening . . ."

She gathered me in her arms like a comforting mother. "It's okay," she said softly. "You just let yourself go for once, and you frightened yourself."

"You mean there's hope for me yet?" I said with an attempt at levity.

"Well, I'm not giving up on you," said Reyne.

CHAPTER ELEVEN

Gerald picked up one of the photographs. He looked at the faded writing on the back. "The Kid and Daddy, eh?"

I continued to shovel the remaining photographs back into the manila envelope. "It seems my father's pet name for me was *The Kid.*"

Sitting down at the opposite side of my desk, Gerald examined the photo closely. "You were too serious even then, Victoria. How old were you here? Six? Seven?"

I held out my hand for the photograph. "Don't know," I said offhandedly. "Probably about six."

He looked at the manila envelope with interest. "Any more of you there?"

"Just old family photos. Nothing of importance."

I felt a tremor of annoyance as Gerald shoved his hands in his pockets and stretched out his lanky legs, seemingly set for a long conversation. "Everything ready for your trip?" he said.

"I *do* have a lot of things to finish up before Friday when I go," I said meaningfully.

Gerald didn't take the hint. "Victoria, I've been thinking about us . . ."

"Yes?"

I thought my tone made it clear that I didn't want to continue the topic, but he went on, "I just want you to know I'm not going to give up." His tone was conversational, but his expression implacable. "I happen to love you." He paused, then added, "Very much."

"I'm sorry, but I don't love you." I felt relieved that I had bluntly stated it, instead of hedging around the subject for fear of hurting him.

He took his hands out of his pockets and sat forward in the chair. "You *think* you don't love me because . . ." He cleared his throat. "You have a bit of a problem with sex. Lots of people do and you can be helped. Please know I understand, and it's okay. We can work on it. I love you and I think we should be married."

Taking a deep breath, I said tightly, "Sex isn't the problem. That isn't the reason I won't marry you."

141

"I can give you so much. And I *need* you."

Feeling my customary impotence to deal with his benign persistence, I said in an even tone, "Gerald, I don't know how I can say this plainly enough for you to believe me, but I love you only as a friend. No more than that."

A shadow of anger passed over his face. "We've slept together as lovers for some time, Victoria. Isn't it a bit late to deny our feelings for each other?"

"I'm not denying *your* feelings, I'm denying that *mine* are what you say. I don't think you'd be happy in a relationship that you gave so much to, and I gave so little."

Now he was angry. "I should be the judge of what would make me happy or not." His expression changed. "Victoria, please . . ." He stood up. "No, don't say anything . . . just think about it."

"I don't need to think!"

He smiled at me bleakly. "Yes, you do, because I'm not giving up. I know there's no one else and the real problem is you're frightened of making a commitment to me. I'll wait as long as it's necessary."

He was at the door before I said, "There is someone else."

He smiled over his shoulder at me. "Good try, Victoria, but we both know there isn't."

It was a frantically busy week as I labored to get everything ready for a colleague to take over during my absence in the United States. I postponed viewing the Super-8 films until just before I left, convincing myself that only pressure of work dictated my reluctance to make time to see them.

Millennium had sent Reyne back to Melbourne because of a furor over rumors that the Vera Eiesley jury had been stacked, the jury selection process manipulated so that a majority was sympathetic to the accused and antagonistic towards the Church. Reyne had called and said she'd be back Thursday, the day before I flew out of Australia.

I was grateful for the buffer of work, which filled my waking hours effectively, although a combination of excitement and consternation over thoughts of Reyne continually leaked into whatever I was doing. I supposed what I felt for her was love, although the feeling was far more uncomfortable than anything I might have imagined. Her absence was a steady ache, and I was alarmed at my growing need to see her.

I slept restlessly, often dreaming of my aunt and uncle's house, or repeating the familiar nightmare of bright lights and shameful nakedness. And there were constant images of Reyne. In dreams I kissed her, made love to her — but I was always aloof, untouchable.

The fact that Aunt Felice had told the inquest one story about my parents' last meeting, and, years later, another version to Zoe, nagged at me constantly. Although I knew it would probably be a futile visit, one afternoon I went to see my Uncle David.

The Good Shepherd retirement home was bleakly unwelcoming as usual. My uncle lay in his narrow bed, his large white hands folded neatly on his stomach, blinking uncomprehendingly as I tried to question him about my father. Locked in the wreckage of his brain might be the answer to why my parents died, and I had to find the key to the memory.

As I'd come in through the chilly entrance to the building, Matron Scott, small but formidable, had stopped me to announce, "The Reverend, your uncle — he's worse. Much worse. Shouldn't be surprised if he didn't see out the month."

Past acquaintance had told me the matron took a grim satisfaction in bearing bad news, so when I asked if he was likely to remember anything from some years ago, she said triumphantly, "*Most* unlikely, Professor Woodson. At the best, a moment, a scene, maybe a name."

So far, the matron had been right. As I talked to him, occasionally Uncle David would turn his head to me as though he had caught sight of something familiar, but most of the time he gazed vacantly ahead.

"Isabelle," I said. "Do you remember your brother's wife?"

"Isabelle?" There was a flash of intelligence. "Isabelle . . . poor Isabelle." His voice became stronger. "She's dead. Gone to hell."

This didn't shock me. Hell and damnation had always been a large part of my uncle's vocabulary. "But why? What did Isabelle do?"

Uncle David looked surprised. "Murder, of course."

The word jolted me like an unexpected punch, but I hurried to take advantage of this moment of clarity. "Who did Isabelle murder?

He turned his head away, mumbling incoherently.

I felt like shaking him, but I said agreeably, "Uncle David, tell me about Isabelle."

"She's gone to hell."

"I know Isabelle's gone to hell. But why has she?"

He looked at me directly, his eyebrows raised. "Why? Because she murdered Frank."

For a moment I felt detached, almost coldly amused. It seemed some ludicrous escalation had occurred. I could hear the explanations, one after the other: *Your mummy and daddy aren't coming back for a while ... Your mother and father have gone to Heaven ... Your parents died in a car crash ... Your parents burned to death ... Your mother deliberately crashed the car to murder your father ...*

Then I found myself seizing him by the shoulders, the words spilling out of me in a desperate stream. "Uncle David! Why? Why would she do that? Tell me! Tell me what you know."

He stared at me stupidly, his head bobbing as I shook him. I released him, horrified at my loss of control.

"Uncle David, I'm sorry. Forgive me ..." Appallingly, his face puckered up like a frightened child's, and I was swept with shame and confusion.

I stayed for a while, patting his hand and talking gently, as if that would make up for what I'd done. "I'll see you soon, Uncle David, when I get back." He watched me warily as I backed out of the room.

Matron Scott was waiting for me. "Well, how was he?"

I had myself well in hand. "Just as you described."

As she nodded her pleasure at this vindication of

her judgment, I said, "My uncle did mention a few things. I'd like to know what weight can be put on what he said."

"You can never tell, really," said the matron firmly. "I mean, some fragments of memory are probably quite accurate. Others ... well! Just imaginings, I'd say."

When Reyne had called to say she was back in Sydney, I suggested we meet in her apartment, since I was sure she must be tired. Her reply made me smile. "I'm coming to *your* place tonight, Victoria, but it's not because of you. Frankly, it's Tao who's won my heart."

I waited with increasing anxiety for her to arrive. I wanted to see her, talk to her, touch her — but not to make love. That would be too threatening, too perilous.

To my astonishment, I realized that I wanted to tell her about Uncle David and my inexplicable loss of control. I'd tried to rationalize what had happened, but my attempts to explain my behavior seemed hollow. And what would Reyne think of what I'd done? Would she find excuses as I was trying to do? *There's no point in telling her. I'm going to put it out of my mind.*

She came through the door with the crackling energy I was drawn to, one hand outstretched with a small package. "I bought you a gift."

My surprise was evident. Reyne's smile melted all

my reserve. "Just something I saw I thought you'd like."

The gift was a beautifully carved wooden cat, sitting in the august pose that Tao often assumed, its sleek arrogance endearing. I turned it in my fingers, enjoying the smooth planes of the heavy wood. "Thank you."

She stood watching me, her expression unreadable. "I want you to be happy," she said.

Impulsively, I put my arms around her. "It's beautiful, Reyne . . . and so are you." I was so embarrassed by the awkwardness of my compliment that I took refuge in a quick kiss.

Reyne put her hand behind my head and gently guided my lips back onto hers. Her mouth was electric, compelling. We kissed with an abandon I never imagined I'd experience. A tide of warmth rose in me, catching at my breath.

"Don't think," said Reyne. "Just feel."

I had to touch her bare skin, make her want me. It was the ability I had to arouse her that was firing my passion. She willingly assisted my clumsy attempts to undress her. "You first," I said. "Please."

As she lay under me on the bed I exulted in my power, my dominance. She moaned at my touch, her nipples hard, thrusting into my palms. And I was drunk with the same need, vibrating with the same longing. She curved against me as my fingers slid into her. "Oh, darling!"

Her words, the wet texture of her, intoxicated me. I moved my hand and she moved with me. I wanted to savor, to store the memory of her body, but I was overcome by a cascade of sensation. My hand caught her rhythm and she rose to the pressure of my fingers. Higher and higher, arched in aching silence for a moment, then shaking with orgasm.

I called out with her: it was the only moment of true oneness I had ever known.

"I can't," I said.

"Darling, don't try so hard."

I turned my face away, miserable in failure. "I'm not trying too hard, Reyne. I just can't."

CHAPTER TWELVE

My flight to Los Angeles didn't leave until mid-afternoon, so I'd postponed my packing until the morning. Reyne, who had an early interview, didn't stay for breakfast. She'd cuddled me all night, and I'd slept, dreamlessly, in her arms. I woke to her sleepy mumblings, and lay still, unable to express in words or actions the dimensions of affection that swelled within me. As we dressed, I was noncommittal, even terse, but she didn't seem to mind. She departed in a swirl of energy, leaving my house depleted by her absence.

I packed with my usual efficient care, then, while it was still early, went to the university. I'd put off viewing the two reels of film to the very last, but I knew I couldn't leave Australia and have their menace still unexplained.

I locked the door of my office behind me and stood like someone about to begin a testing race. Ted, an assistant from the university library, had put the Super-8 projector on my desk with a note attached explaining the intricacies of loading the film, but before I set it up I took out the envelope with my father's business papers. I remembered from my first cursory glance a few mail order catalogs for Woodson Enterprises' films, and I hoped to find some connection to these two films. I leafed through the documents until I found the catalogs stapled together.

The first pages covered the categories I expected — training and education — but at the back was a separate page headed *Very Private Entertainment*. I had to force myself to look at the titles. Clearly they were pornographic films, many imported from Scandinavian countries. At the bottom a short list was sub-headed *Homegrown Australian Fun*. I cringed at the titles: *The Kid Loves Daddy, Daddy's Little Girl, The Kid is Hot.*

When I tipped the two innocuous yellow film containers onto my desk I sat and stared at them. Wouldn't it be better if I never knew what was on them? They couldn't be what I suspected. It wasn't possible. I could hear my breath singing in my ears as I picked up the first one, *K5 plus* and loaded it into the projector.

The film began with me as a little girl sitting

naked on a bunny rug, blinking in the harsh light pouring in from some source outside the frame. I looked small and puzzled, especially when a male hand began to give me a selection of "toys" to play with. As I watched, my heart began to race with forgotten terror when I saw my five-year-old self crying as the vibrator was inserted into me.

If the first film stunned me, the impact of the second one, *K & FW*, was far greater. I felt physically ill as I watched the frames chatter through the projector. Presumably someone else operated the camera as my father, naked, took me on his lap. I was wearing a little dress with brightly colored flowers. He cooed to me, caressed me, encouraged me to play with his stiffening penis. Then he undressed me in a mockery of a striptease until I stood naked between his knees . . .

The inscriptions my father had scrawled on the containers were now clear: *K5 plus* meant *The Kid aged five plus sex toys; K & FW* meant *The Kid and Frank Woodson.* I wished he were still alive, so I could howl my outrage at him, flay him with words as my mother must have done.

I was so sick with revulsion that I could barely dial Zoe's number. When she answered with her usual abruptness, I said without preliminaries, "Zoe, I've just seen the films that were in the box of papers that you gave me. Did you have any idea what was on them?"

"I wasn't sure, Victoria . . . but Mum —"

I broke in, fierce with pain. "You told me you didn't know why my parents were fighting, but it was because my mother found out, wasn't it?"

Zoe's voice was subdued, sympathetic. "Victoria, I

didn't tell you because I couldn't. And it was better that you never found out."

"Then why give me the papers? Why give me the films?"

Her voice was sharp with self-justification. "I didn't look through the box. I didn't know what was there." She paused, then said more moderately, "But of course, I guessed. I suppose I . . . wanted to leave it up to you. I wasn't sure what Mum told me was true — and I didn't really want to know."

I shut my eyes, thinking of the conspiracy of silence that had enveloped me. "Does John —"

"No. Mum made me promise not to tell him."

"Whatever you promised, you have to tell *me*."

Zoe hesitated, then said quickly, "Don't blame Mum, Victoria. Just before she died she said again she was still sure it was best you were never told about the films."

My voice was harsh. "My father used me to make money from child pornography. Don't you think I have a right to know that?" I took a ragged breath, my self-possession dissolving in grief. "Shouldn't I know that pedophiles watched me . . ."

"Oh, Victoria, I'm so sorry."

I realized with a shock that Zoe was crying too.

"What can I do?" she sobbed.

"Nothing. There's nothing anyone can do." I forced myself to sound calmer. "I'll just have to cope with it, that's all."

After I hung up I sat staring stupidly at the phone, my will paralyzed. A phrase from somewhere kept repeating in my head: *The truth shall set you free.* Would that happen? Was I free now of the power of the searing memories whose pain had made my mind blot them out of existence?

I thought of Reyne, of calling her ... and my heart rebelled. Last night I couldn't tell her how I'd lost control with my Uncle David — so how could I tell her *this*? What I had to do was think it through, put some order on the chaos of my thoughts and feelings, reestablish myself at the quiet center again.

Gerald had insisted that he drive me to the airport, even though I told him not to bother. I felt drained, exhausted, yet guilty that I didn't want his company. We exchanged desultory conversation in the car and while I was checking my luggage. Then we faced each other with nothing to shield our differences.

"Gerald, I haven't been fair to you."

"I understand."

I gazed at his familiar, thin face, and knew that I was going to hurt him irrevocably. "It's wrong of me not to have said this earlier, but I was fooling myself, as well as you."

His expression changed, as though he realized that these were not my usual half-hearted denials. "Victoria, I —"

"Recently, I've found out a lot about myself, about why I am the way I am. I can't love you. I never will be able to love you — not the way you have every reason to expect."

"I can accept that."

"But *I* can't, Gerald. I'd be miserable, knowing you wanted, and needed, so much more than I can give you. I can't marry you . . . will never marry you. It would be a lie to let you think there was any chance at all."

He looked away from me, rubbing his fingers across his forehead. "*Is* there someone else?"

I felt overwhelmingly weary. "It doesn't matter if there is, or isn't. Please understand. It would make no difference." I blinked at my sudden tears. "I never meant to hurt you this way."

Gerald took a deep breath, and when he looked at me there was resignation on his face. "So that's it?"

"I'm sorry . . ." I stopped at the inadequacy of my words. He nodded, as though I'd completed the sentence.

Hugh had watched our exchange from a distance and when Gerald kissed my cheek, then turned and walked away, he hurried over. "Gerald isn't waiting until we board?"

I wiped my hands across my cheeks. "Obviously not."

Quantas Flight Eleven droned its way across the Pacific, chasing time as we crossed the International Date Line. We'd left Sydney mid-afternoon Friday: we'd arrive in Los Angeles near ten o'clock in the morning of the same day.

Hugh, sitting next to me in Business Class, glanced anxiously at me from time to time, particularly when I ordered my fourth gin and tonic. "Victoria, is something wrong?"

"Nothing's wrong."

"You don't look yourself, you don't look yourself at all." He pursed his lips. "I imagine you're worried about the tour and I'm pleased to go through the itinerary with you. It's going to be a great success —"

I broke in with brutal frankness. "Hugh, don't talk to me. I need silence. All right?"

He nodded reluctant agreement. "Okay, but . . . you're not ill, are you?"

"I'm fine. I just need to be left *alone*."

As Hugh settled back in his seat, grunting unhappily, I considered that last emphatic word. Alone — I was *alone*. Who could, or would, or would want to — share my loneliness? I knew, intellectually, that I was not to blame for what had happened to me. I'd had a child's trust in my father to love me and protect me. It was not my fault that he'd abused that trust.

I put my head back and closed my eyes, listening to the reassuring dull rumble of the engines. The meaning of my recurring dream of bright lights and shame at my nakedness was no longer mysterious. But was knowing the truth enough to change a lifetime of narrow, safe responses?

I'd put the envelopes containing the contents of the box in my luggage. When I could bear to, I intended to sort through them carefully, looking at everything in the light of what I now knew. I wondered at what point my mother had begun to suspect. She'd worked for an office employment agency in the city, and, as my father's registered office was our home address, I'd have often been in his sole care.

Scenarios ran through my mind: had my mother come home unexpectedly and interrupted a film session? Or had she seen my father's pet name for me in the catalog and screened one of the films out of curiosity? Had I been present when she accused my father, and been ashamed because *I* was the cause of their rage against each other? In my imagination I could see the images she must have gazed at with the same horror that I had experienced.

Was this the reason that my mother had crashed the car and killed them both? Had my Uncle David been right when he said Isabelle had murdered — executed — my father? Would she have done that, even if it meant dying herself? Or had she intended to discuss everything rationally, then become so upset, so angry, that she'd lost concentration and plowed into the tree?

Fatigue from the twelve or so hours in the air had dulled the sharpness of my emotions, so I walked off the plane like an obedient automaton, following Hugh's exhortations without question. I collected my luggage and stood waiting in line for the legality of my entry into the United States to be established with an official stamp from the Immigration Service.

Hugh clucked impatiently at the logjam caused by a tour group with inappropriate visas, but I was beyond caring about such trivialities. My new knowledge was forcing my whole view of myself to shift and realign. Explanations and reasons for what I was and how I behaved were changing, but were not yet in clear focus.

When we finally reached our hotel — "One of the best in L.A." Hugh assured me — I told him I had to call Australia on a personal matter, and would meet the charge on the hotel bill.

Hugh was patently curious. "If all you want to do is tell someone you've arrived safely, I can do that for you when I'm ringing my office." He checked his watch. "Well, not yet, of course, since in Australia it's still *very* early in the morning."

"I need to make the call myself, Hugh."

Alone in the understated luxury of my hotel room, I sat on the edge of the bed puzzling over the instructions for international calls. After the long flight I wanted a long, hot shower, but much more important was my need to speak with Reyne. As I acknowledged that need, I had the sweet realization that I was totally certain she would welcome my call, even if I woke her from sleep.

The connection was clear, as if we were only a short distance apart, not thousands of miles. My heart turned at the pleasure that warmed her voice. "Hi. I was going to call your hotel a little later."

I smiled. "Were you?"

"Of course. I intend to chase you by telephone across the States until we meet in New York."

I bit my lip as tears stung my eyes. Her affection had broken through my artificial calm. When I didn't respond to her comment, she said, "Hey — are you still there?"

157

I cleared my throat. "I'm here."

Her voice suddenly gentle, she said, "Something's wrong, isn't it? Tell me."

Immediately after viewing the films in my office, I'd been in a panic of humiliation and confusion, needing to keep secret from Reyne what I'd discovered. Now that I'd managed to get the flood of my thoughts into perspective, I wanted to tell her because — I realized with a jolt — she was the person I felt closest to, safest with. "I've found out something about my father . . ."

The words came tumbling out. I explained, described, my voice staccato with stress. She didn't interrupt as I struggled to express what I thought and felt.

When I had finished, she said, "Oh, darling . . ."

In the past, I'd never sought comfort, priding myself on my stoicism, but at that moment I wanted Reyne to hold me and tell me everything was all right. It took a moment until I realized she was asking me something. "I'm sorry?"

"I said, do you want me to come to the States early? I'll rearrange my schedule."

"For me? Would you do that?"

"Of course." Reyne sounded surprised that I'd asked the question.

I wanted to know why I meant so much to her that she would do such a thing. What was so special in me that she couldn't find it in someone else? I said, "Thank you Reyne. It means so much to me that you're offering to do that, but you know Hugh has every waking moment filled, and as long as I see you in New York . . ."

Long after we'd broken the connection, I sat

mesmerized by the possibilities that a future with Reyne might hold. Yet underneath that thread of hope was my fear that I could never be sufficient for her happiness ...

I'd been to the United States before on sabbaticals, visiting various universities and centers of learning, but show business American-style was an entirely new world to me. Everything seemed to be brighter, harder, more intense. In talk shows I found myself asked astonishingly frank questions — by Australian standards — about my personal life. In self-defense I swiftly developed a safe set of answers, but I continued to be amazed by the intimate details other people being interviewed would reveal.

Hugh shadowed me everywhere, assessing the attentions of people in entertainment or publicity who seemed to sense, like leeches, the dollar possibilities of new blood. The tour was turning out to be a much greater success than I'd anticipated. Although Hugh was obviously hoping Rampion Press would ascribe this to his efforts alone, I suspected it was more an accident of timing. Apart from the benefit of my exotic Australian accent and citizenship of a country widely regarded as strange and wonderful, it was fortunate that I didn't have competition from some famous author publicizing his or her latest book. In addition, we'd only just arrived in the States when a controversy erupted about "pornography" in literature being introduced in university study programs, and I found myself the instant expert on the topic.

I was bitterly amused at the fine literature that was being defined as pornography. The bigots who condemned the celebration of desire between adults ignored the *true* pornography in society, the exploitation of women and children like me in print and film — and in the home — where we were *victims,* not equal participants.

I spent two hectic weeks of interviews, plane flights and anonymous hotel rooms in one city after another. Apart from appearances, I avoided socializing with Hugh or Rampion executives as much as possible, preferring to spend the time alone in my room. Once Reyne was in New York, I established a routine of speaking with her every evening. Strangely, I felt closer to her on the telephone than I did when we'd been together. I grew skillful in assessing the tone of her voice, the nuances of her words. Day by day she became more important to me, and I looked forward to our meeting in New York with a mixture of trepidation and happiness.

I could be rational about my sexual coldness. It was obviously related to repressed childhood memories of my father's abuse, and then the loss of my parents — my mother. I smiled wryly to myself. The chilly upbringing I'd experienced with my aunt and uncle could not have helped, either.

But logic could only take me so far. I wanted to believe — I hoped with something close to desperation — that understanding what had happened to me would be enough to change me.

I kept returning to one thought. Reyne . . . would it be different with Reyne?

CHAPTER THIRTEEN

I barely had time to check the room's layout and the spectacular New York skyline through the hotel window before the phone rang. I snatched up the receiver, hoping to hear the warmth of Reyne's voice.

"Victoria? It's Zoe. I got your number from your publishers."

Surprised to hear her brusque tone, I said, "Is something wrong?"

"No. Nothing's wrong." The distinct time lag as our voices leaped the circuit to the satellite then back to earth gave our conversation a quality of dislocation.

I was about to ask why she was calling when she said, "I suppose you wonder why I'm calling."

I was puzzled by her tentative manner. It was so unlike Zoe to be indirect.

"The fact is, Victoria, I've been thinking about you. About your father and what you found out . . ."

I felt suddenly trapped in the brightly lit cell of the hotel room. "Who have you told?"

"I haven't told anyone." She sounded puzzled. "Why would I?" She didn't wait for an answer. "I'm calling because I'm worried about you. I want to know if you're all right."

The genuine concern in her voice broke through my reserve. Out of a surge of affection came an unexpected desire to be open. "Zoe, I can still hardly believe those awful things happened to me. I don't remember them. I've seen the films, I know I was abused. Even so, my memory's still a blank."

"Mum and Dad — they should have done something."

I found myself in the unusual position of defending my aunt and uncle. "They *did* do something — they gave me a home."

Zoe made an impatient sound. "Fine, Victoria, but Mum and Dad knew what happened to you, so why didn't they arrange counseling, something to help you . . ."

I felt the anguish of the past well up in me. "I don't know why they didn't, Zoe. Perhaps they thought it was best forgotten."

"Maybe it would be better if you'd never found out."

"No!" My response was involuntary, intense. "I have to understand what happened to me in the past ..."

Zoe's sigh came gusting down the line. "But knowing it has upset you so much."

I was impatient with her. "I can recover from *that* pain, because I know what causes it ..." I searched for words to make it clear — to myself as well as Zoe. "My life's been twisted by things I can't remember, but they still have the power to damage me. I need to know what they are, so I can cope with them."

"Is that why you wrote the book?"

Her question took me by surprise. "The book?" I repeated.

Her sympathetic tone dissolved in mercurial anger. "*The Erotic Muse,* of course. It's all about sex, isn't it? I've often asked myself why you, of all people, would write such a thing."

I managed a derisive laugh. "I had the time to write about it because I wasn't *doing* it, Zoe."

In the silence that followed, the international line crackled softly. Then, meekly, Zoe said, "I'm sorry, Victoria. The last thing you need is me attacking you over your book." Then, in a tone clearly demonstrating that we were to move to safer subjects, she continued, "And how's New York?"

We chatted for a few moments more, and, as we were ending our conversation, I said, "Zoe, I've decided that if Arthur brings in a business manager, I'll be happy to invest in his company."

This didn't bring the pleased response I'd expected. "You're not saying that because ... I was nice to you?"

"No, unexpected though it was."

Zoe laughed at my tart tone. "Oh, good," she said, "because it's quite unlikely to happen again."

Having a couple of hours to spare before Hugh picked me up for a luncheon appearance, I showered, wrapped myself in a toweling robe, and stretched out on the bed's pale green quilt. I'd left a message for Reyne at the *Millennium* offices, and I hoped she'd call back before Hugh arrived. In the meantime, I intended to put my mind in neutral and sink into a pleasant doze.

But my mind refused to wind down. My thoughts spun in a whirlpool of pictures, snatches of conversation, sharp emotions. I could feel my fingers digging into Uncle David's shoulders as I shook him, see my father's smiling face in the film, hear my aunt's cold voice criticizing me for some transgression. I turned to bury my face in the pillow. If I couldn't control this torrent of images, how could I ever be whole?

Abruptly, my memory threw up a conversation I'd had with Gerald: I stood in my kitchen glaring at him as he said with aggravating assurance, ". . . why not consider therapy?" And then, after my furious response, "It could give you some insight . . ."

I opened my eyes. *You're a victim of incest,* an inner voice said. I sat up. "No, I'm not," I said aloud. "My father made films of me, that's all."

But was that all? And weren't the films made for men to find pleasure in the things my father did to me? Suddenly resolute, I swung my legs over the edge of the bed. If I denied the actuality of my father's offenses against me, I'd be repeating what I'd done for so many years — hiding from the truth.

The ringing phone broke into my thoughts. "Hi!" said Reyne.

"Oh, darling ..." I stopped, disconcerted by my use of an endearment. I made an absurd effort to explain. "Actually, I don't call people darling ..."

"I should hope not."

I tried to match her light tone. "It must have slipped out because I'm quite fond of you."

"That accounts for it," said Reyne agreeably.

We made arrangements to meet. The first opportunity would be late that night, since Reyne had a full day of appointments and I had a dinner where I was to give a talk titled, *Erotica — the Sex Drive Tamed?* My address originally had a rather more mundane title, but some publicist had changed it, and, as Hugh pointed out, "Who cares what it's called, as long as they come to see you?"

As I hung up, there was a peremptory knock. "Victoria? You ready?"

"Hugh," I said, opening the door a crack, "you're not going to believe this, but I'm running a little late ..."

Reyne was staying in the Greenwich Village apartment of a work colleague who was overseas on assignment. I insisted that I would come to her, using the excuse of wanting a change from the sameness of hotel rooms. The real reason was that I knew if we were to have an equal relationship it had to be based on equality, and that meant I had to put myself out for Reyne, rather than always expect her to fit in with me.

Late Friday night in New York was exhilarating. The buildings, the lights burning in empty offices, thrust themselves into a sky made pale with the glow of the city, as people and vehicles poured through the streets in impatient streams. The doorman of the hotel where my dinner engagement had taken place imperiously beckoned one of the ubiquitous Yellow Cabs and handed me into it. The vehicle was noisy with radio music, grubby, and driven by a bearded man with a well-developed death wish. As we joined the lurching traffic to honk our way to the Village, I found myself enjoying the maelstrom of sound and activity. The city was alive with a vibrancy that made me tingle with a matching energy.

Reyne had been watching for my cab and came down to greet me. She was dressed in jeans and a T-shirt, and I felt over-formal in my lime-green dress. Her smile was broad as she said, "I hope you notice I hurried right down. Don't want any good-looking New York woman whisking you away."

I smiled at her, delighted by the actuality of her presence. She'd been so close to me for weeks — in my thoughts, on the telephone — but now I could touch her, see her cool expression fired by the warmth of her smile, taste her mouth . . .

"I'm so pleased to see you." I knew I sounded awkward and over-careful.

She gave me a quick, tight hug. "Called anyone else *darling*, today?"

"No."

"Lucky for you!"

The apartment had a shabby, clean comfort that relaxed my formality. I sat in a well-worn leather chair and grinned up at her. "I was on a TV panel show this afternoon," I said. "And we were discussing, of all things, sex." I shook my head. "You wouldn't believe the other panelists!"

"Yes I would. This is New York and anything goes."

I was suddenly solemn. "Do *we* go, Reyne?"

"Together, you mean? I think we do."

"There are some things you should know . . ." I stopped, defeated.

Reyne took my hand, linking our fingers. "There's no hurry."

I was driven by a compulsion to confess. "I didn't mention it, but I saw my Uncle David before I left. He's in a nursing home. He's bedridden and he doesn't remember very much." I bit my lip. "Reyne . . . I shook him when he wouldn't tell me what I wanted to know."

She tightened her fingers. "You're going through a tough time."

I wanted more than the comfort of her words. "Can we go to bed?"

She grinned at me. "I was rather thinking of supper, first — but if you insist . . ."

I lay on my back staring at the patterns of light on the ceiling. "Reyne, I'm not enough for you."

She stretched lazily against me. "You're what I want."

"Will you always be content with *this*?"

The light from the street outside was enough to illuminate the serious lines of her face. "It's going to take a long time, Victoria."

The memory of my failure raw, I said caustically, "What? For me to have an orgasm?"

"For you to heal."

Provoked, I pulled myself away from her and sat up. "I'm all right."

"During the last couple of weeks I've seen a couple of people, asked some questions —"

"About me?" Fury made my voice thick. "Am I one of your projects, now?"

Her voice was quiet. "You're a victim of incest."

I got out of the bed, swearing as I stumbled over my discarded clothes. "I can cope with it. Everything happened a long time ago, and my father's dead. I have to get on with my life."

Reyne snapped on the bedside lamp and sat blinking in the glare. "Most incest victims need professional help to get over the trauma."

"I don't!"

She shocked me with her sudden anger. "I love you, Victoria, but I don't relish the thought of being tied to someone who needs help and won't accept it."

Rage burst through my controls. "Jesus, Reyne! *I'm* the victim, not you."

She smiled at me ruefully. "Right now, I'd say we both are."

CHAPTER FOURTEEN

Hugh was enthusiastic about the final day's program. I was too, for a different reason. I'd be spending four days free in New York with Reyne, who was also taking a break before returning to Australia. Hugh rushed me through the revolving doors of the hotel and into a cab — fully as yellow and as dirty as the one the night before.

The first item on our schedule was a visit to the offices of Rampion Press. As our cab joined a traffic jam, Hugh said, "They've put a larger-than-life photograph of you up in the lobby." His manner was that of one who had achieved this coup single-handed.

"Should I be impressed?"

"Well, of course you should, Victoria! The company only does that for *major* authors."

In the afternoon rain began in fitful heavy showers. To add to the discomfort, a vicious, gusty wind sprang up. My last official duty was a radio interview, and afterward I insisted on walking the three or four blocks back to my hotel, no matter how unpleasant the weather. "I need to clear my head, Hugh. And it doesn't matter if I catch cold now. The tour's over."

I strode along the sidewalk, hands jammed into the pockets of my coat, enjoying my freedom, enjoying the cold wetness against my face. My thoughts revolved around Reyne. Last night we'd gone back to bed with our conflict apparently resolved, but I hadn't slept well. I'd lain awake for hours, listening to Reyne's even breathing.

Back in my hotel room, as I showered, then put on jeans and a deep pink silk shirt I'd bought during the tour, I rehearsed what I'd say.

Reyne was early. She came in laughing, but I was determined not to be deflected. "Reyne, about last night . . ."

"Last night was fine. We were together."

"Not together enough. When we make love I get so close . . . and then I can't. I'm sorry, Reyne."

She brushed my cheek with the back of her hand. "Why are you apologizing?"

I shrugged. Not wanting to endure her steady

gaze, I walked over to the window and feigned interest in the New York skyline.

Reyne said, "You don't have to prove anything to me. I love you."

"*Why* do you love me?"

She moved behind me to look over my shoulder at the canyons of the city. "There's the Chrysler Building. Great, isn't it?"

"You're not going to answer me?"

She pressed against my back, locking her arms about my waist. She whispered against my neck, "I love you because you're a fine, lovable person, but mostly because you're you." She nibbled at my ear lobe. "And, of course, because I can't help it."

It was as though everything suddenly clicked into place. I wanted to say something significant, something to fix this moment as the one where I had begun to accept Reyne's love unconditionally — to stop worrying why she could love me, and just accept that she did. My career was based on words, but I could find none to express the exultation that rose in me. I had begun to tremble, and she raised her head.

"Victoria?"

In answer I took Reyne's locked hands and slid them down my stomach. Her fingers curled against the seam of my jeans, the pressure translating into a pounding ache. She freed one hand and slid it under my shirt. Gasping as she touched my breasts, I turned my head in hunger for her mouth.

"There's no hurry," she breathed.

The heat throbbed in me. "There is!"

171

I turned in her arms until I could seize her in a hard embrace. My mouth was open for her kiss, eager for the thrust of her tongue. It wasn't enough — I had to be free of all barriers, to have Reyne's skin against mine.

Clumsy with urgency, we discarded our clothes. I whimpered as her palms brushed my thighs. The ache had become a torrent of exquisite pain that buckled my knees. Still locked in a kiss, we sank onto the softness of the bed. She was above me, the weight of her breasts cupped in my palms. I rose up to meet her, one arm around the curve of her back, the other hand plunging into the heat between her legs.

She threw back her head with an inarticulate cry, the sound releasing in me a surge of joy that had to find words.

"Reyne, I love you."

I gloried in the rhythm of my hand that had the power to flood her with such burning delight. As she vibrated against my fingers, my passion rose to match hers, but I couldn't follow her as she spilled over into orgasm.

Her release was my agony. I seized her hands. "Please!"

She was cruel, merciless. "Not yet." She caressed me, gentle as I shivered with the need for force. She slid down my body, her breath hot against my skin, pushed my knees wide. Then her mouth was savoring my swollen flesh.

I was arched, the breath caught in my throat, sensation spilling in molten drops, then concentrated, tightening in a noose of ecstasy.

A cry burst from me as I thrashed with the

jolting shocks that rolled in wave after wave, until I lay breathless, half-laughing, half-crying.

Reyne kissed me gently as I lay smiling in her arms.

"You know," I said, "I think I could grow to like that . . ."

Publications from
BELLA BOOKS, INC.
The best in contemporary lesbian fiction

P.O. Box 10543, Tallahassee, FL 32302
Phone: 800-729-4992
www.bellabooks.com

WHEN LOVE FINDS A HOME by Megan Carter. 280 pp. What will it take for Anna and Rona to find their way back to each other again?   1-59493-041-4 $12.95

MEMORIES TO DIE FOR by Adrian Gold. 240pp. Rachel Katz, a forensic psychologist, attempts to avoid her attraction to the charms of Anna Sigurdson. Will Anna's persistence and patience get her past Rachel's fears of a broken heart?   1-59493-038-4 $12.95

SILENT HEART by Claire McNab. 280 pp. Exotic lesbian romance.
                                                                    1-59493-044-9 $12.95

MIDNIGHT RAIN by Peggy J. Herring. 240 pp. Bridget McBee is determined to find the woman who saved her life.   1-59493-021-X $12.95

THE MISSING PAGE A Brenda Strange Mystery by Patty G. Henderson. 240 pp. Brenda investigates her client's murder . . .   1-59493-004-X $12.95

WHISPERS ON THE WIND by Frankie J. Jones. 240 pp. Dixon thinks she and her best friend, Elizabeth Colter, would make the perfect couple . . .   1-59493-037-6 $12.95

CALL OF THE DARK: EROTIC LESBIAN TALES OF THE SUPERNATURAL edited by Therese Szymanski—from Bella After Dark. 320 pp.   1-59493-040-6 $14.95

A TIME TO CAST AWAY A Helen Black Mystery by Pat Welch. 240 pp. Helen stops by Alice's apartment—only to find the woman dead . . .   1-59493-036-8 $12.95

DESERT OF THE HEART by Jane Rule. 224 pp. The book that launched the most popular lesbian movie of all time is back.   1-1-59493-035-X $12.95

THE NEXT WORLD by Ursula Steck. 240 pp. Anna's friend Mido is threatened and eventually disappears . . .   1-59493-024-4 $12.95

CALL SHOTGUN by Jaime Clevenger. 240 pp. Kelly gets pulled back into the world of private investigation . . .   1-59493-016-3 $12.95

52 PICKUP by Bonnie J. Morris and E.B. Casey. 240 pp. 52 hot, romantic tales—one for every Saturday night of the year.   1-59493-026-0 $12.95

GOLD FEVER by Lyn Denison. 240 pp. Kate's first love, Ashley, returns to their home town, where Kate now lives . . .   1-1-59493-039-2 $12.95

RISKY INVESTMENT by Beth Moore. 240 pp. Lynn's best friend and roommate needs her to pretend Chris is his fiancé. But nothing is ever easy.   1-59493-019-8 $12.95

HUNTER'S WAY by Gerri Hill. 240 pp. Homicide detective Tori Hunter is forced to team up with the hot-tempered Samantha Kennedy.   1-59493-018-X $12.95

CAR POOL by Karin Kallmaker. 240 pp. Soft shoulders, merging traffic and slippery when wet . . . Anthea and Shay find love in the car pool. 1-59493-013-9 $12.95

NO SISTER OF MINE by Jeanne G'Fellers. 240 pp. Telepathic women fight to coexist with a patriarchal society that wishes their eradication. ISBN 1-59493-017-1 $12.95

ON THE WINGS OF LOVE by Megan Carter. 240 pp. Stacie's reporting career is on the rocks. She has to interview bestselling author Cheryl, or else! ISBN 1-59493-027-9 $12.95

WICKED GOOD TIME by Diana Tremain Braund. 224 pp. Does Christina need Miki as a protector . . . or want her as a lover? ISBN 1-59493-031-7 $12.95

THOSE WHO WAIT by Peggy J. Herring. 240 pp. Two brilliant sisters—in love with the same woman! ISBN 1-59493-032-5 $12.95

ABBY'S PASSION by Jackie Calhoun. 240 pp. Abby's bipolar sister helps turn her world upside down, so she must decide what's most important. ISBN 1-59493-014-7 $12.95

PICTURE PERFECT by Jane Vollbrecht. 240 pp. Kate is reintroduced to Casey, the daughter of an old friend. Can they withstand Kate's career? ISBN 1-59493-015-5 $12.95

PAPERBACK ROMANCE by Karin Kallmaker. 240 pp. Carolyn falls for tall, dark and . . . female . . . in this classic lesbian romance. ISBN 1-59493-033-3 $12.95

DAWN OF CHANGE by Gerri Hill. 240 pp. Susan ran away to find peace in remote Kings Canyon—then she met Shawn . . . ISBN 1-59493-011-2 $12.95

DOWN THE RABBIT HOLE by Lynne Jamneck. 240 pp. Is a killer holding a grudge against FBI Agent Samantha Skellar? ISBN 1-59493-012-0 $12.95

SEASONS OF THE HEART by Jackie Calhoun. 240 pp. Overwhelmed, Sara saw only one way out—leaving . . . ISBN 1-59493-030-9 $12.95

TURNING THE TABLES by Jessica Thomas. 240 pp. The 2nd Alex Peres Mystery. *From ghosties and ghoulies and long leggity beasties . . .* ISBN 1-59493-009-0 $12.95

FOR EVERY SEASON by Frankie Jones. 240 pp. Andi, who is investigating a 65-year-old murder, meets Janice, a charming district attorney . . . ISBN 1-59493-010-4 $12.95

LOVE ON THE LINE by Laura DeHart Young. 240 pp. Kay leaves a younger woman behind to go on a mission to Alaska . . . will she regret it? ISBN 1-59493-008-2 $12.95

UNDER THE SOUTHERN CROSS by Claire McNab. 200 pp. Lee, an American travel agent, goes down under and meets Australian Alex, and the sparks fly under the Southern Cross. ISBN 1-59493-029-5 $12.95

SUGAR by Karin Kallmaker. 240 pp. Three women want sugar from Sugar, who can't make up her mind. ISBN 1-59493-001-5 $12.95

FALL GUY by Claire McNab. 200 pp. 16th Detective Inspector Carol Ashton Mystery. ISBN 1-59493-000-7 $12.95

ONE SUMMER NIGHT by Gerri Hill. 232 pp. Johanna swore to never fall in love again— but then she met the charming Kelly . . . ISBN 1-59493-007-4 $12.95

TALK OF THE TOWN TOO by Saxon Bennett. 181 pp. Second in the series about wild and fun loving friends. ISBN 1-931513-77-5 $12.95

LOVE SPEAKS HER NAME by Laura DeHart Young. 170 pp. Love and friendship, desire and intrigue, spark this exciting sequel to *Forever and the Night.*
ISBN 1-59493-002-3 $12.95

TO HAVE AND TO HOLD by Peggy J. Herring. 184 pp. By finally letting down her defenses, will Dorian be opening herself to a devastating betrayal?
ISBN 1-59493-005-8 $12.95

WILD THINGS by Karin Kallmaker. 228 pp. Dutiful daughter Faith has met the perfect man. There's just one problem: she's in love with his sister. ISBN 1-931513-64-3 $12.95

SHARED WINDS by Kenna White. 216 pp. Can Emma rebuild more than just Lanny's marina? ISBN 1-59493-006-6 $12.95

THE UNKNOWN MILE by Jaime Clevenger. 253 pp. Kelly's world is getting more and more complicated every moment. ISBN 1-931513-57-0 $12.95

TREASURED PAST by Linda Hill. 189 pp. A shared passion for antiques leads to love.
ISBN 1-59493-003-1 $12.95

SIERRA CITY by Gerri Hill. 284 pp. Chris and Jesse cannot deny their growing attraction . . . ISBN 1-931513-98-8 $12.95

ALL THE WRONG PLACES by Karin Kallmaker. 174 pp. Sex and the single girl—Brandy is looking for love and usually she finds it. Karin Kallmaker's first *After Dark* erotic novel.
ISBN 1-931513-76-7 $12.95

WHEN THE CORPSE LIES A Motor City Thriller by Therese Szymanski. 328 pp. Butch bad-girl Brett Higgins is used to waking up next to beautiful women she hardly knows. Problem is, this one's dead. ISBN 1-931513-74-0 $12.95

GUARDED HEARTS by Hannah Rickard. 240 pp. Someone's reminding Alyssa about her secret past, and then she becomes the suspect in a series of burglaries.
ISBN 1-931513-99-6 $12.95

ONCE MORE WITH FEELING by Peggy J. Herring. 184 pp. Lighthearted, loving, romantic adventure. ISBN 1-931513-60-0 $12.95

TANGLED AND DARK A Brenda Strange Mystery by Patty G. Henderson. 240 pp. When investigating a local death, Brenda finds two possible killers—one diagnosed with Multiple Personality Disorder. ISBN 1-931513-75-9 $12.95

WHITE LACE AND PROMISES by Peggy J. Herring. 240 pp. Maxine and Betina realize sex may not be the most important thing in their lives. ISBN 1-931513-73-2 $12.95

UNFORGETTABLE by Karin Kallmaker. 288 pp. Can Rett find love with the cheerleader who broke her heart so many years ago? ISBN 1-931513-63-5 $12.95

HIGHER GROUND by Saxon Bennett. 280 pp. A delightfully complex reflection of the successful, high society lives of a small group of women. ISBN 1-931513-69-4 $12.95

LAST CALL A Detective Franco Mystery by Baxter Clare. 240 pp. Frank overlooks all else to try to solve a cold case of two murdered children . . . ISBN 1-931513-70-8 $12.95

ONCE UPON A DYKE: NEW EXPLOITS OF FAIRY-TALE LESBIANS by Karin Kallmaker, Julia Watts, Barbara Johnson & Therese Szymanski. 320 pp. You've never read fairy tales like these before! From Bella After Dark. ISBN 1-931513-71-6 $14.95

FINEST KIND OF LOVE by Diana Tremain Braund. 224 pp. Can Molly and Carolyn stop clashing long enough to see beyond their differences? ISBN 1-931513-68-6 $12.95

DREAM LOVER by Lyn Denison. 188 pp. A soft, sensuous, romantic fantasy.
ISBN 1-931513-96-1 $12.95

NEVER SAY NEVER by Linda Hill. 224 pp. A classic love story . . . where rules aren't the only things broken. ISBN 1-931513-67-8 $12.95

PAINTED MOON by Karin Kallmaker. 214 pp. Stranded together in a snowbound cabin, Jackie and Leah's lives will never be the same. ISBN 1-931513-53-8 $12.95

WIZARD OF ISIS by Jean Stewart. 240 pp. Fifth in the exciting Isis series. ISBN 1-931513-71-4 $12.95

WOMAN IN THE MIRROR by Jackie Calhoun. 216 pp. Josey learns to love again, while her niece is learning to love women for the first time. ISBN 1-931513-78-3 $12.95

SUBSTITUTE FOR LOVE by Karin Kallmaker. 200 pp. When Holly and Reyna meet the combination adds up to pure passion. But what about tomorrow? ISBN 1-931513-62-7 $12.95

GULF BREEZE by Gerri Hill. 288 pp. Could Carly really be the woman Pat has always been searching for? ISBN 1-931513-97-X $12.95

THE TOMSTOWN INCIDENT by Penny Hayes. 184 pp. Caught between two worlds, Eloise must make a decision that will change her life forever. ISBN 1-931513-56-2 $12.95

MAKING UP FOR LOST TIME by Karin Kallmaker. 240 pp. Discover delicious recipes for romance by the undisputed mistress. ISBN 1-931513-61-9 $12.95

THE WAY LIFE SHOULD BE by Diana Tremain Braund. 173 pp. With which woman will Jennifer find the true meaning of love? ISBN 1-931513-66-X $12.95

BACK TO BASICS: A BUTCH/FEMME ANTHOLOGY edited by Therese Szymanski— from Bella After Dark. 324 pp. ISBN 1-931513-35-X $14.95

SURVIVAL OF LOVE by Frankie J. Jones. 236 pp. What will Jody do when she falls in love with her best friend's daughter? ISBN 1-931513-55-4 $12.95

LESSONS IN MURDER by Claire McNab. 184 pp. 1st Detective Inspector Carol Ashton Mystery. ISBN 1-931513-65-1 $12.95

DEATH BY DEATH by Claire McNab. 167 pp. 5th Denise Cleever Thriller. ISBN 1-931513-34-1 $12.95

CAUGHT IN THE NET by Jessica Thomas. 188 pp. A wickedly observant story of mystery, danger, and love in Provincetown. ISBN 1-931513-54-6 $12.95

DREAMS FOUND by Lyn Denison. Australian Riley embarks on a journey to meet her birth mother . . . and gains not just a family, but the love of her life. ISBN 1-931513-58-9 $12.95

A MOMENT'S INDISCRETION by Peggy J. Herring. 154 pp. Jackie is torn between her better judgment and the overwhelming attraction she feels for Valerie. ISBN 1-931513-59-7 $12.95

IN EVERY PORT by Karin Kallmaker. 224 pp. Jessica has a woman in every port. Will meeting Cat change all that? ISBN 1-931513-36-8 $12.95

TOUCHWOOD by Karin Kallmaker. 240 pp. Rayann loves Louisa. Louisa loves Rayann. Can the decades between their ages keep them apart? ISBN 1-931513-37-6 $12.95

WATERMARK by Karin Kallmaker. 248 pp. Teresa wants a future with a woman whose heart has been frozen by loss. Sequel to *Touchwood.* ISBN 1-931513-38-4 $12.95

EMBRACE IN MOTION by Karin Kallmaker. 240 pp. Has Sarah found lust or love? ISBN 1-931513-39-2 $12.95

ONE DEGREE OF SEPARATION by Karin Kallmaker. 232 pp. Sizzling small town romance between Marian, the town librarian, and the new girl from the big city. ISBN 1-931513-30-9 $12.95

CRY HAVOC A Detective Franco Mystery by Baxter Clare. 240 pp. A dead hustler with a headless rooster in his lap sends Lt. L.A. Franco headfirst against Mother Love.
ISBN 1-931513931-7 $12.95

DISTANT THUNDER by Peggy J. Herring. 294 pp. Bankrobbing drifter Cordy awakens strange new feelings in Leo in this romantic tale set in the Old West.
ISBN 1-931513-28-7 $12.95

COP OUT by Claire McNab. 216 pp. 4th Detective Inspector Carol Ashton Mystery.
ISBN 1-931513-29-5 $12.95

BLOOD LINK by Claire McNab. 159 pp. 15th Detective Inspector Carol Ashton Mystery. Is Carol unwittingly playing into a deadly plan? ISBN 1-931513-27-9 $12.95

TALK OF THE TOWN by Saxon Bennett. 239 pp. With enough beer, barbecue and B.S., anything is possible! ISBN 1-931513-18-X $12.95

MAYBE NEXT TIME by Karin Kallmaker. 256 pp. Sabrina has everything she ever wanted—except Jorie. ISBN 1-931513-26-0 $12.95

WHEN GOOD GIRLS GO BAD: A Motor City Thriller by Therese Szymanski. 230 pp. Brett, Randi, and Allie join forces to stop a serial killer. ISBN 1-931513-11-2 $12.95

A DAY TOO LONG: A Helen Black Mystery by Pat Welch. 328 pp. This time Helen's fate is in her own hands. ISBN 1-931513-22-8 $12.95

THE RED LINE OF YARMALD by Diana Rivers. 256 pp. The Hadra's only hope lies in a magical red line . . . climactic sequel to *Clouds of War*. ISBN 1-931513-23-6 $12.95

OUTSIDE THE FLOCK by Jackie Calhoun. 224 pp. Jo embraces her new love and life.
ISBN 1-931513-13-9 $12.95

LEGACY OF LOVE by Marianne K. Martin. 224 pp. Read the whole Sage Bristo story.
ISBN 1-931513-15-5 $12.95

STREET RULES: A Detective Franco Mystery by Baxter Clare. 304 pp. Gritty, fast-paced mystery with compelling Detective L.A. Franco. ISBN 1-931513-14-7 $12.95

RECOGNITION FACTOR: 4th Denise Cleever Thriller by Claire McNab. 176 pp. Denise Cleever tracks a notorious terrorist to America. ISBN 1-931513-24-4 $12.95

NORA AND LIZ by Nancy Garden. 296 pp. Lesbian romance by the author of *Annie on My Mind*. ISBN 1931513-20-1 $12.95

MIDAS TOUCH by Frankie J. Jones. 208 pp. Sandra had everything but love.
ISBN 1-931513-21-X $12.95

BEYOND ALL REASON by Peggy J. Herring. 240 pp. A romance hotter than Texas.
ISBN 1-9513-25-2 $12.95

ACCIDENTAL MURDER: 14th Detective Inspector Carol Ashton Mystery by Claire McNab. 208 pp. Carol Ashton tracks an elusive killer. ISBN 1-931513-16-3 $12.95

SEEDS OF FIRE: Tunnel of Light Trilogy, Book 2 by Karin Kallmaker writing as Laura Adams. 274 pp. In Autumn's dreams no one is who they seem. ISBN 1-931513-19-8 $12.95

DRIFTING AT THE BOTTOM OF THE WORLD by Auden Bailey. 288 pp. Beautifully written first novel set in Antarctica. ISBN 1-931513-17-1 $12.95

CLOUDS OF WAR by Diana Rivers. 288 pp. Women unite to defend Zelindar!
ISBN 1-931513-12-0 $12.95